S.P. Peredo is a Mexican-American pathologist who has traveled extensively and has lived in many places within the United States, his native Mexico, and Canada. Peredo has published a fair number of scientific articles, including a poem on his thoughts while performing an autopsy, but this is his first work of fiction. He has compiled a volume of poetry and is hard at work on additional short stories, a movie screenplay, and his autobiography. S.P. Peredo presently lives in Mission, Texas.

To Masha, Sigmund, Sebastian, Sammy, Camila, and Gali – the six reasons why I wake up grateful to have seen the light of another day – and to my granddaughters, Crista and Vida, for existing.

S.P. Peredo

Marco's Journey and Other Stories

Austin Macauley Publishers™
London • Cambridge • New York • Sharjah

Ordering Information:
Quantity sales: special discounts are available on quantity purchases by corporations, associations, and others. For details, contact the publisher at the address below.

Publisher's Cataloging-in-Publication data
Peredo, S.P.
Marco's Journey and Other Stories

ISBN 9781643782157 (Paperback)
ISBN 9781643782164 (Hardback)
ISBN 9781645367185 (ePub e-book)

Library of Congress Control Number: 2020900704

www.austinmacauley.com/us

First Published (2020)
Austin Macauley Publishers LLC
40 Wall Street, 28th Floor
New York, NY 10005
USA

mail-usa@austinmacauley.com
+1(646)5125767

Table of Contents

Marco’s Journey

“If you begin your journey to Ithaca,
ask that the road be a long one,
full of experiences and knowledge.”
– Konstantino Kavafis

1

Marco Rosen woke suddenly to the strong vibrations of a boom, followed ominously by a loud, clanking noise. His head was still leaning against the airplane window, and for two seconds upon opening his eyes thought, absurdly, that he was piloting a fighter jet that had just broken the sound barrier. Then he remembered he was a passenger on a Mexicana Airlines flight from Mexico City to Tuxtla Gutiérrez that had made a scheduled stop in Villahermosa, Tabasco.

He was so tired that he had fallen asleep while the plane was barely departing the terminal for the second leg of the journey. But the plane had blown out one of its engines so it was now reluctantly taxiing back to let its passengers off.

"Damn it!" he muttered angrily when the captain informed them what had happened. They were going to disembark and wait; hopefully, there would be another airplane they could use, if not they would be stranded until tomorrow.

The whole trip had been terrible from the beginning. He had been late getting to the airport because of the insane Mexico City traffic and had boarded barely on time, agitated and sweating after having run the entire length of the endless terminal corridors lugging a suitcase and a brief case, each growing heavier by the minute. He got on as the crew was about to close the door. He was panting and trying to ignore everyone's dirty looks as he worked his way down the aisle to his seat between a rather large gentleman and a young mother carrying a baby. Worse yet, there had been no chance of changing seats afterward; the plane was entirely full!

And now this; a broken-down plane. This glitch in his plans would make it difficult for him to reach Tuxtla Gutiérrez in time. The following morning, he was going to deliver a lecture at the 1989 Annual Chiapas Medical Society meeting. It was to be a magisterial speech highlighting his medical research on uterine cervical cancer that spanned two years of arduous work; it was innovative and hopefully might even catch the eye of the international scientific community, especially the Americans and Europeans who always seemed reluctant to publish research from Latin America. He pondered this as he sat back in the uncomfortable airport chair to wait.

The worst part of the trip, however, had been the fretful, sleepless night before. Belina, his wife, had confessed she no longer loved him and that, despite fifteen years of marriage and two children, she could no longer see anything positive about staying together. She informed him that when he returned, she would not be at home, would temporarily move in with her parents. "I need to find myself," she added.

What does that even mean when someone says they must 'find' themselves? He wondered. *What actually is lost? Your soul? Your mind?* Marco guessed this was a euphemism for: 'I am dissatisfied with my life and must make a change in order to find happiness.'

He had sensed Belina's unhappiness many times. Once, she had even gone as far as to say she resented the fact that she had given up her dreams to help him pursue his.

So, now he was struggling to see in what way he might have contributed to the demise of their marriage.

It was true he had finished his education and had gotten his medical degree while she had quit school when she got pregnant, but he had not asked her to quit. And it hadn't been easy for him either; part-time jobs, staying up late (sometimes all night) to study, barely functioning, all the energy drained.

It was true he had become a 'workaholic,' and had largely neglected her and the kids for his own personal gain. He was driven, almost blindly; late night research sessions, preparing lectures, redoing experiments, tweaking variables, analyzing and reanalyzing results, writing papers.

It was also true that he had a bad temper, hating to be interrupted by her or the kids just when his concentration had led him to an apex, a breakthrough, a 'Eureka' moment, as they say. He thought of the time he had lost it nearly to the point of insanity when Marquito and Mario, his twin boys, had spilled juice on a manuscript that he was putting the finishing touches on. He had made them cry. But once he had calmed down, he had to admit it had been his fault. Served him right for doing work next to two six-year-olds as they ate their waffles and orange juice.

Then there was that affair he'd had (and by golly, what an affair!) with Isabel, the grad student with green eyes and a figure that pressed against her clothes which she always wore too tight, even her lab coat (especially her lab coat!). He had driven her home, after the retirement party for Dr. Cordoba, both of them with a little too much champagne on board, and one thing led to another, as they say (another phrase meant to expunge responsibility from what you have done). He had regretted it later – although neither right away nor completely – after Belina had found out and confronted him about it.

Marco was feeling confused and exhausted, a combination that always creates numbness, a sense of defeat in a losing battle against the oppressions of life. But why did it have to be this way if he was successful in every way society – that absurd product of human evolution – had established?

Belina's timing couldn't have been worse. He was reaching a milestone in his career, but he had pain that made it impossible for him to savor it, mainly because he still loved Belina, or so he thought. Nevertheless, the idea of losing her created a gnawing pressure in his chest.

Was this feeling, that at once was bad and good, bittersweet, so to speak, natural to love? He was surprised to realize that he was feeling it for the first time in his life.

These were the thoughts that ebbed in his mind as he sat there amongst strangers in that uncomfortable airport chair. Feeling lonely and misunderstood, he had closed his eyes in an effort to avoid a conversation, not out of shyness, but rather out of the need to ruminate, wallow in his painful contemplations.

And he had fallen asleep.

Suddenly, he felt a hand on his shoulder, and once again, Marco woke to a fleeting fantasy. This time, in the two seconds after opening his eyes, he saw a crowd of ravishingly beautiful people: Men dressed in tails and white tie, hair slicked back, sporting Clark Gable mustaches, and elegant women in glamorous evening gowns, wearing tiaras studded with sparkling gems on their immaculately coiffed hair. All wore white gloves that muffled their applause as they smiled, all eyes on him. Was that the king of Sweden touching his shoulder?

And then he realized, sadly, he was still in the dimly lit, damp terminal of the Villahermosa airport, and someone he didn't know was talking to him enthusiastically.

2

Basilio Borja was one of those aggressively happy people that always seems to be present whenever difficult situations arise. He was a businessman who had experienced, given his many travels, similar circumstances, and he said to Marco, paraphrasing John Lennon with excessive optimism, “There are no problems, amigo, but only solutions.” Upon hearing that no plane would be available until the following day, Basilio had taken it upon himself to negotiate a ride with one of the airport shuttle drivers. Once he was off work, the driver had said he would be willing to take him in the airport van all the way to Tuxtla Gutiérrez but he needed six people to make it worth his while. He would be charging one thousand pesos each, he had added. So, Basilio began recruiting riders. By the time he approached the slumbering Marco, four other people had already agreed.

“How long will it take?” asked Marco.

Basilio explained that they would have to ride up into the mountains and through a forest so thick and forbidding it was called the Black Forest, and they would be riding on a twisting road with patches still unpaved.

“So, a trip that by air is slightly under one hour, by land becomes a journey of five to six hours.”

He further informed Marco that it all depended on the conditions of the road, and that the weather was often capricious in those parts, a sunny day suddenly becoming cloudy, leading to a surprisingly torrential rainfall.

"But," Basilio assured, "this will probably not happen since it is November, amigo, and such erratic behavior of the clouds occurs mainly in the summer months."

Marco felt he had no choice. If he waited until the next day, he could give up all hope of making it on time. Six hours seemed okay, he figured. It was already 3:00 pm, but even a late arrival to his hotel would afford him sufficient time to rest and be ready for his presentation.

"Alright, I'll go."

Once they had handed over their money, they were led by the driver, a middle-aged, unsmiling but polite fellow named José, to the van he had parked outside the main entrance. It was a white Volkswagen minibus, a 'Combi' as they were known. The emblem of the aviation federation was emblazoned on the front doors. The two back rows of seating had been placed facing each other. Marco got in first and ended up sitting directly behind the driver, facing backwards. Once the other passengers had taken their seats, José got in behind the wheel and started the engine. He gave them a barely audible summary of the journey ahead as he put the van into gear.

The obligatory introductions began as they rocked to and fro with the movement of the van. Marco hated this; hated being forced to talk to complete strangers. But he also knew there was no way to avoid it if he was to share such a long ride with them.

Basilio Borja once again took the lead and introduced himself. He was a chubby, middle-aged man with dirty glasses and a pencil-thin mustache. He was wearing a khaki, one-piece jumpsuit that by now exhibited sweaty armpits and a grimy collar. This didn't seem to bother him as he spoke through that perennial smile of his.

Next, the man facing Basilio said his name was Pedro Nucamendi. As it turned out, the person sitting between him and Marco was his younger brother, Pablo. Marco pondered on the similarity of the brothers who could have been twins. Both were handsome with dark hair, cut in a similar manner, olive skin and fairly light brown eyes. If they had said they were Spaniards or Italians, Marco would have believed them. But they were not; they were native. "Chiapanecos, and proud of it," Pedro said.

It was now Marco's turn. Reluctantly, he stated his name and nothing more. The rest looked around at each other but did not insist, given the unfriendly look on Marco's face that had registered as arrogance. Instead, since it seemed they were proceeding counterclockwise, they fixed their gaze on the man sitting in front of Marco.

He was someone Marco had noticed instantly upon arrival at the terminal. He was tall with fair skin, nearly white blond hair and astonishingly pale blue eyes. An American, Marco had thought at first; but on closer inspection had ruled that out because he was casually but sharply dressed and had a quiet, unassuming manner. Scandinavian? Perhaps. Then the man solved the issue; his name was Rainer Saller, from München, Germany.

A polite silence ensued, some of them quietly nodding, impressed that he spoke Spanish so remarkably well.

Mexicans are always curious about foreigners, and for some reason feel the need to speak to them. “Welcome to our group of travelers,” Basilio said, with exaggerated courtesy.

The person sitting between Rainer and Basilio now spoke without being prompted to do so. His name was Pánfilo Herrera López, originally from the State of Tabasco but now living in Tuxtla Gutiérrez.

Rainer and Pánfilo could not have been more opposite in appearance. While Rainer could epitomize a character out of a novel about Teutonic knights, Pánfilo could have been drawn from the stele of a Mayan pyramid; he was short with tan skin, straight black hair and eyes so dark they appeared to sparkle as he looked this way and that.

All this transpired in the twenty minutes or so the van wrangled its way through the city traffic. Finally, they reached the last Pemex filling station where they stopped for gas before taking Highway 195 out of the city.

3

The grocery store was across the highway and Marco could see Pedro, Pablo and Basilio working their way across the parking lot back to the van. Pedro and Basilio were each carrying a cardboard box loaded with things while Pablo was huffing along with a wooden 24-pack of medium-sized Coca-Colas.

As José had pulled up to the gas pump, they had volunteered to go purchase 'essentials for the trip.' Marco assumed they wanted to buy snacks and drinks for the road, so like the others, he handed over his contribution of one hundred pesos.

At last, they were off.

Not ten minutes had passed when the straight road through battered fields of dry grass and dirt began to wind through lush, grassy hills. It was that time of day when the angle of the autumn sun illuminated the green, green grass with a bright yellow hue in such a way that it seemed almost on fire. Half an hour later, the climbing began, up into mountainous woodlands, the palm trees having ultimately given way to tall, deciduous trees, many with twisted branches that cast spooky silhouettes against the dazzling, bluish-pink sky. All six passengers were silent as if mesmerized by the beauty of the land.

Marco was starting to feel thirsty so he turned his attention to the boxes where he could see an assortment of items. One box contained all sorts of chips, packs of chocolate cupcakes, small pineapple pies and a stack of plastic cups. A bottle of Presidente brandy and another one of white Bacardi rum stuck out from the top of the other box that also contained a bag of ice cubes.

He regretted that he had not gotten out of the van to drink some water when he had the chance, but the thought of a Coke with lots of ice appealed to him, so he asked if he might have some, intending to serve himself. Pablo smiled at the request, seeming to appreciate the opportunity to begin the day's libations.

"Please, allow me to prepare your drink," Pablo said.

Marco watched as Pablo poured a sizeable portion of rum over the ice cubes quite deftly, given the movement of the van, without spilling a drop. He then topped it off with Coke. Out of nowhere, he produced a lemon wedge, the juice of which he squeezed into the drink, completing the 'cuba libre.'

Marco had not intended to drink alcohol; he was a bad drinker, with a known vulnerability to hard liquor. But he accepted it out of courtesy and was glad he did, because once everyone else had been served their drinks, and had toasted a hearty 'salud' to the trip still ahead, and 'to friendship,' Basilio had added, he felt the first, cold swallow almost tingle in the back of his mouth. And the delicious, tenuous sweetness of the rum and Coke combined with the tangy lemon juice created an unexpected, almost sensuous feeling as it made its way down to his stomach. By the third swallow, he began to relax.

"This is delicious," he said to Pablo. "I've never had a better drink in my life. A bartender could not have made it any better."

Now Pedro smiled and said, enthusiastically, "Ah, you see, amigo, my kid brother, Pablo, *is* a bartender and, I might add, the best in the whole world."

He then went on to explain that ever since they were very young, their family owned a restaurant, and they had grown up learning how to cook, wait on tables, charge customers, wash dishes, and prepare cocktails. Their mother had been the main cook until the business became so busy that they had to employ other people to help. After they had finished school, Pedro in business administration and Pablo in tourism and hotel management, they had enlarged the restaurant and it became a huge success. It was now one of the most popular spots for dining and entertainment in downtown Tuxtla. They had even added live music on the weekends, mostly with local bands, but sometimes had enough money to contract famous groups and entertainers, "such as Ricardo Montaner and Maná," he added, almost swollen with pride.

"You must come see us whenever you are in town. It's called 'Restaurant Las Brasas.'"

The drinks began to flow freely.

José dutifully refused to drink anything other than soda, stating that it was his responsibility to deliver the six gentlemen safely to their destination.

“So, please, you enjoy the ride. I am quite content to be at your service.”

Everyone now had begun to lose their inhibitions.

4

About an hour into the trip, someone needed to go to the bathroom. When the van pulled over, the six got out, with much fanfare, laughing and remarking wittily, as men often do when they are drinking.

To the right of the van, there was a high wall of rock that had been carved to create the highway. Marco could see vegetation peeking out from the edge as he looked straight up, almost wrenching his neck. To the left of the van, there was a precipice, a shear drop to an idyllic scene of endless green far below. Remarkably, cows that seemed the size of ants were grazing, apparently on their own since no humans were in sight within the enormous space that stretched to the horizon.

The six men stood shoulder to shoulder and urinated in unison on that wall of rock. Rainer let out a prolonged sigh. “Oh, I feel so free!” he exclaimed with eyes closed, face up, taking in the double pleasure of relieving his bladder while feeling the gentle breeze full of the whispers of the mountains.

Back in their seats and after the van had gone through some curves in the road, they once again entered a heavily wooded area. Rainer began to speak once more; his gaze and mind seemed lost deep in the forest.

“Near my home in Germany, there is also a Black Forest. I love the darkness of those woods, and the way the light filters in poetic streams through the trees, creating a wondrous place, much like this, where we Germans feel at home.” Still looking out, he continued, “We are forest people. The forest, with its foliage, its animals – yes, even its mythical creatures – is part of our essence.”

All were pondering what he had said, momentarily silenced by Rainer’s easy eloquence.

Basilio asked Rainer, not with his usual assertiveness but gently, with true interest, what he did for a living and why he had decided to visit Mexico, thinking that Rainer possibly was a writer or an artist.

“I am a lawyer,” Rainer said. “I work as a prosecutor for the courts back home.” He then proceeded to tell the story of why he was traveling.

5

Two years earlier, his daughter, Hansi, had died. She was twenty years old and was coming home from school for Christmas. The problem was she was bringing home her boyfriend, Walther, a guitar player that had dropped out of school to start a rock band and pursue his dream of being a professional musician. Rainer did not approve of him; he had forgotten, he supposed, what it was like to be young and willing to take on the world.

He also couldn't remember, he thought in retrospect, when he had become the ogre of a father he had sworn never to be. He had been, after all, liberal and rebellious in his youth; his father had reprimanded him harshly, at times asking him to 'stop being a bum.' Rainer didn't detect at what point in his life his insensible transformation occurred. Suddenly, he was an adult and arguing with his daughter over her boyfriend and ignoring the fact that she was in love.

"You know how it is for a father. No man seems good enough for your little girl."

He regretted it now, because his intransigence had created months of strife that also had repercussions on his marriage; his wife, Dora, had not been so quick to judge their only child.

Rainer and Hansi had argued before her trip began. Ironically, he couldn't remember now exactly why. He didn't know how her state of mind had been while driving and if it contributed to the accident, but she lost control of her little car on the snowy, icy autobahn and crashed violently against a tree. Hansi and Walther were pronounced dead at the scene by the emergency personnel.

"It seems quite telling that they were found locked in an embrace."

"Dora never recovered emotionally. How could she? Is there any greater pain for a mother?" he asked, his eyes becoming red and humid as he invoked the memory.

"She never forgave me, nor can I forgive myself. I carry around the enormous burden of guilt within my heart, much like the mariner his albatross."

Six months after the accident, Dora left him and went to live in the isolated summer cottage they owned in Bavaria. No amount of pleading on Rainer's part could persuade her to return.

Rainer had tried to work, hoping that through total immersion in his job, he could find even a semblance of tranquility. "What an illusion it was to think this. No manner of distraction can ever serve to erase such pain," Rainer said.

Eventually, he told his coworkers that he needed some time off and decided he would come to Mexico, a land that he had always admired because of its remarkable history and majestic geography, but mainly because of its magic.

"It seemed to me the logical place to be, given my state of mind, a place imbued in magic and where pain – the pain of conquest that merged two disparate worlds – had given rise to a nation of unlimited creativity and art."

"I was hoping this beautiful land, and its beautiful people, would turn my pain once again into something productive," he added with regret.

So, he had crossed into Mexico from California and had been working his way down, intending to travel the entire length of the country, something that after nine weeks on the road, he had almost accomplished.

Now, with Rainer putting his hands to his face in an attempt to hide his tears, all fell silent upon hearing his words. Only the movement of the van and the noises of the road prevailed as he lowered his head timidly.

Rainer felt a little tired, but oddly relieved. Generally, a reserved man – it was unusual for him to open up about private, profoundly personal issues – he had finally found a way to break down the enormous levies that held back a great river of emotions that now could flow freely, thanks to the confidence afforded him by this unusual group of companions.

For several kilometers, no one spoke until Rainer looked up again and met Marco's eyes.

"You, Marco, are not from around here either, right? Your name is also German, is it not?"

Marco was still feeling a bit shy, mainly because he was also someone who treasured his privacy. But he answered Rainer with a smile.

"My grandfather was from Germany. He immigrated to Mexico at the turn of the century," Marco said. "He married a Mexican woman and had many children."

“My father spoke a little German but was not really fluent by any means. By the time I came along, the language and traditions had virtually disappeared from our family.”

Looking around at his fellow passengers one by one, Marco proceeded to tell them his story.

6

His grandfather was an uneducated man but had many skills, and eventually established himself as a photographer in the center of Mexico City, a business that he passed down to Marco's father. But Marco, the oldest of three boys and always good in science, had been more interested in pursuing a career in medicine. His father, the good-natured soul he was, understood his son, wishing him only happiness, so he did not oppose his decision. Besides, Marco's siblings had been more than willing to lend their father a hand.

"It was in my first year at the university that I met Belina, oddly enough at my aunt's funeral."

Marco's aunt had been a lifelong friend of Belina's mother, so he wondered why they had never met her before. He had felt attracted to her that day; by the way she paused before speaking, rolling her eyes up for a second as she gathered her thoughts, then going on, with a smile and dimples in her cheeks. He had also admired her hips, how they clung to her black skirt, and how she looked in that white blouse that insinuated small, shapely breasts; the first and second buttons were open, exposing the smooth, young skin of her chest.

They married a year later. The courtship had been a whirlwind of pleasant moments. But the promises had turned out to be false because Marco had been difficult to live with from the beginning, he now admitted. He told them about his painfully deep reflections back at the airport when he had revealed to himself, for the first time, his true nature: the overly ambitious Marco; the profoundly selfish Marco.

"She has decided to leave me, and my life now seems to have lost its purpose."

Basilio, nodding pensively, said, "You are too hard on yourself, amigo. Perhaps she is also thinking about it as you are and will come to her senses once you have been away for a while. Sometimes a little separation is good for a relationship."

Basilio raised his cup, and with a flare of drama, proposed a toast to Rainer and Marco. "Here's to recapturing lost love!"

And they all raised their cups in response.

7

It was now dark as they entered Teapa, more or less the halfway point of their journey.

The town appeared abandoned as they made their way through the empty streets except for the occasional lone figure that would appear suddenly, looking ghostly in the beams of the van's headlights. Up ahead, Marco could see the bright lights of a restaurant, the music becoming louder as they approached.

"La Parrilla Norteña," José informed them. "It's the only place to get a decent meal in this town."

The ambience was thick; stuffy air full of cigarette smoke and the cacophony of loud laughter and clinking glasses. The musicians, a norteño band, stepped through a sad song with an incongruously lively rhythm. Marco recognized the song; ironically, it was about a man attempting reconciliation with his lost love! Was it a sign? He dismissed the thought, surprised that it could have occurred to him, the scientist!

They waited for about ten minutes at the entrance until a pretty girl with braids showed them to their table, thankfully, Marco thought, far from the band.

The meal revived their spirits. They ate northern style tamales, pozole and black beans accompanied by dark

Montejo beer. Someone also ordered a large plate of grilled beefsteak tacos in flour tortillas, the staple of northern Mexican cuisine, that they all shared.

The band took a break and many of the customers had left so they were able to speak without yelling. Marco figured that he wasn't the only one who had observed that Pánfilo, throughout the entire trip, had not touched a drop of alcohol.

"You do not drink, do you, Pánfilo?" he asked.

Pánfilo, half smiling, confessed he was a recovering alcoholic.

8

He was the youngest of many children of a poor farmer from a village near Cárdenas, Tabasco. They subsisted by growing corn and beans and raising chickens. His mother, a skillful seamstress, sold her humble tapestries in the market or repaired clothes for the wealthier women in town. His three sisters had married by age fifteen, and one by one his four brothers had moved to the banana plantations or the city to work in the factories.

"I was semiliterate," Pánfilo said, "having completed only the second grade in the little rural school of our village and without any skills. My father, ill from heart failure, asked me to leave. I was seventeen years old and had lost touch with my siblings."

Pánfilo had wandered for a while and eventually found a job in a gas station where he worked for tips. For a year, he lived at the edge of town in a tiny shack he built himself out of canes with palm branches for a roof. At night, he would steal bananas from a nearby plantation and sell them in the market when he would get out of work. There, he met Mariana, a pretty sixteen-year-old who worked part-time for a lady that prepared meals in a market stall.

Pánfilo and Mariana fell in love and found a small dwelling near the market where they lived in utter poverty. But they were happy.

A year later, their son, Teodoro, was born.

"A beautiful baby with rosy, cherublike cheeks." Sighing, he went on to say, "We were immensely happy with our son and loved him to a degree we never suspected was possible."

Then one awful day, when Teddy, as they called him, was six months old, he developed a fever. Pánfilo and Mariana didn't know what to do and there was no one to guide the young parents. They tried their best to handle the situation on their own, recalling the home remedies their own mothers would use when they were sick. But the fever did not break and three days passed for them in extreme desperation as they watched their little son's life begin to fade away.

So, they went to see a local doctor, a simple country doctor who, nevertheless, was efficient, giving the boy an injection and providing free samples of medicine as well as instructions on how to keep the baby hydrated.

"Don't worry," the doctor had said, with kindness. "Pay me whenever you can. Just follow my instructions and the baby shall be fine."

Exhausted, but with hope, they put the baby in bed with them that night, as if the closeness of their bodies would afford a magic of its own. They fell asleep instantly, never suspecting what would happen next. Mariana, in her fatigue, had slept so soundly she did not feel when she rolled over on little Teddy. When she woke, half his body was wedged underneath hers; he was not breathing and his skin was a pale purple. She screamed and began to sob uncontrollably as she held her lifeless child in her arms.

"Mariana never recovered her sanity."

Pánfilo went on, clearly moved by having recalled this painful time in his life. "A month after the burial, I came home to find her hanging from a wooden beam, a tight rope around her neck, her face the same purple as Teddy's had been. She had left a note asking God to forgive her, but 'all I want is to see my baby' it said.

"I wandered again after that, barely eating, just drinking. The mezcal created a burning inside that provided a small sense of comfort and dulled my mind."

Pánfilo continued, "This would be the way I would die, I had decided, suffering slowly, since I didn't have the courage take my life rapidly like Mariana had."

How it happened, he didn't know, especially since he had been wandering aimlessly and was drunk all the time, but he ended up in his home village. Sadly, he discovered his parents had passed away and his family's house had burned down. No one ever knew why.

"It was Father Ramiro, the village priest who saved me."

The good priest had found him at the church door unconscious and dying, lying in a pool of vomit and blood, he had soiled his trousers. For nearly two years, Father Ramiro nursed him back to health; he fed him and consoled him, freeing him slowly, not towards death as Pánfilo had wished, but back to life, and the pain eventually began to subside.

Pánfilo lived during that time in a small room behind the church and slept on a cot made of rope. That is the time he discovered the pleasure of reading books. First, he read the Bible with Father Ramiro's help, then one by one, he devoured all the books the wise and studious clergyman kept in his study. He loved reading Alexander Dumas and Victor Hugo, Jules Verne, Carlos Fuentes, Jorge Luis Borjes. He read Irving Stone's *Lust for Life* in two days. They would discuss the books after dinner, sometimes until late at night, with lively discussions of the characters and plots, and Pánfilo came to cherish these moments. He helped Father Ramiro by becoming his assistant when mass was held, and he maintained the church, scrubbing the floors, whitewashing the walls, polishing the statues.

But Father Ramiro was very old and one day died while officiating the church service; he simply slumped down and fell to the floor, already dead. A heart attack, they presumed.

A new priest was coming, so Pánfilo left town, taking with him Father Ramiro´s books in a donkey-drawn wagon he purchased with money he had saved.

"I would take a peso here, a peso there from the church offerings. I figured God would forgive me if I someday put it to good use," he said.

Pánfilo again wandered. He traveled through all the villages and towns, selling his books. Frugality had been one of the great lessons from Father Ramiro and it served him well in this journey; by the time he had sold all the books, he had some money, a modest sum by most standards, but still more than he had ever had. He encountered much hardship, eating little, sleeping wherever he could find shelter from the elements, but now the suffering served a purpose, that of self-discovery and atonement. There was no exact plan, but he felt he had to succeed for Father Ramiro. And for Mariana and Teddy.

When he was nearly in San Cristobal de las Casas, he sold the donkey and cart, and bought a bus ticket to Tuxtla Gutiérrez because he had heard from another traveler that there was a book wholesaler there.

He invested all his money in a market stall to sell books. His enthusiasm in reading was unlimited and he often initiated discussions of plots and characters, made recommendations to customers, much as Father Ramiro had with him. Soon, he became known as 'the Bookman.'

"Even teachers would consult with me when creating their lesson plans or ask me to specially order books for them," Pánfilo said. "So, I decided to open up a full-fledged bookstore and found the perfect place for it in the city center. I also found the perfect name for it: 'Libros Matera,' a pneumonic for the three people I have loved most in my life."

"I traveled this week to Villahermosa because I was able, after much inquiring, to contact my siblings. It turns out they had also been searching for me all these years. So, now my brother Raymundo and I are contemplating the idea of opening a second book store there."

"But I apologize for having made my story so lengthy. I know we must be on our way," said Pánfilo.

"And an amazing story it is, albeit sad, amigo," retorted Basilio. He paused, then continued. "I actually have been to your bookstore. Why, just last week..." Basilio was interrupted by a ruckus across the room.

9

Several men were trying to subdue a drunk who was yelling loudly, saliva spurting from his lips, contorting to free himself, and looking their way.

He stumbled hurriedly towards their table, knocking down chairs; he seemed to be pointing at Basilio, calling his name and cursing at him with abundant profanity. In one final lunge, he was upon him. Basilio never saw the punch coming, a big fist smashing into his face, his glasses flying upwards in pieces. He stumbled backwards, falling to the floor, incredulous and dumbfounded.

Rainer and Pedro joined in the effort to restrain the man, and finally, they were able to usher him out into the street where his companions drove him away and out of sight.

Marco immediately hurried over to Basilio and examined him. He was dazed but conscious and bleeding from a gash across the bridge of his nose and left eyebrow. Applying pressure with a clean napkin, Marco helped Basilio to his feet. Leaning on Marco's shoulder, he walked slowly to the van, looking down, too embarrassed to look forward.

"Who is that man?" asked Marco.

“My ex brother-in-law,” replied Basilio. He hesitated before explaining. “He has never forgiven me for cheating on his sister. We got a divorce because of it.”

“Did that happen recently?” asked Marco, not being judgmental, but just trying to understand what could have provoked such a display of anger.

“It happened about seven years ago,” Basilio said.

“That seems like an awfully long time to hold such a grudge,” Marco exclaimed.

Basilio hesitated again but went on. “The problem, Marco, is that I didn’t cheat on her with another woman, but with another man.”

10

They were on the highway again. Luckily, José had a first-aid kit, and by the time Marco had finished dressing Basilio's wound, they had crossed the line into the State of Chiapas, and Basilio had a black eye!

Basilio took a big shot of brandy, straight, no ice, no Coke, savoring it with closed eyes as it burned his lips, tongue and throat. He needed to explain.

"I studied in the normal school in Tuxtla Gutiérrez and became a teacher," he began. "I later went on to finish a master's degree and taught math at preparatory school level."

That's where he met Adela, a quiet and shy geography teacher. They were compatible in many ways and they became the best of friends, spending most of their free time together; going to dinner, the movies, late night cooking, family outings, laughing. Everyone assumed one day they would marry, and they did.

Until then, they had never been intimate. Oh, they hugged and kissed, sometimes even passionately, but they had never slept together, even that time Basilio had stayed overnight at her house. He was very tired, he remembered telling her. Besides, he believed a man and woman should not have sexual relations until they were married, or so he would say, and they didn't.

"You see," Basilio said, shyly, "the excuses I gave Adela were false. The fact is, as you all already suspect, that I was struggling, and had always struggled, with the fact that I am attracted to men."

But Basilio's father had been a stern, inflexible man. And as it often happens when one grows up, whether gay or straight, with a tyrannical father, there is a continuous, futile and exhausting effort to please him, gain his recognition, even late into adulthood.

"But I discovered over time, that the conflict is mainly within oneself, and sadly, doesn't end until someone dies. And if it's your insensitive father that dies first, you never stop feeling guilty about the fact that you are relieved that he's dead."

Basilio went on, "If he had died before I took the worst way possible to prove to him, and myself, that I was not gay, in other words, before I married a woman who didn't deserve for that to happen, I wouldn't have married Adela."

"Don't get me wrong," Basilio tried to clarify, "Adela is a wonderful, intelligent woman, and a man – any man – would have been happy, lucky, to have her as a wife. And even after marrying her, I tried to live up to her expectations, and worse, my father's expectations. But after a while, I couldn't make love to her without feeling terrible about how I had screwed up my life, and worse, her life."

The story became even more complicated as Basilio went along.

Adela's father was a wealthy widower who owned two department stores. Shortly after Adela and Basilio married, he died, leaving one of the stores to Adela in his will.

The other store, owned and managed by Carlos, Adela's brother (the man who had punched Basilio in the restaurant), was on the verge of bankruptcy due mainly to his incompetence.

Adela's store, on the other hand, was thriving due to the fact that Adela had the vision to ask her husband, who was a math whiz, for help. They had both quit their teaching jobs and gambled their careers in order to make the store prosper as it had when Adela's father, a very competent and shrewd businessman, had managed it.

Basilio talked to Carlos and convinced him to merge the stores into one company, a brand new one that they could even rename, "Tiendas Benjamín," he suggested, in honor of his late father-in-law, and they did.

"Both stores did very well, with a common management, or should I say, with me overseeing the management. But Carlos, despite my warnings, and crazed by the sudden surge in profits, began a careless lifestyle of womanizing and partying. It became a gargantuan effort for me, now with only minimal participation on his part, just to keep the businesses afloat."

"And then I met Hermilo," Basilio shrugged, a hint of embarrassment on his face. "He is an Adonis," he said, half smiling, looking down. Then, collecting himself, went on. "He was a trainer at the Toro Gym where I had gone to enquire about membership. I had decided I was going to lose these extra pounds," he mentioned as an aside, thumping his belly.

The day he met Hermilo, Basilio knew he could no longer live with the profound and perennial feelings of foreboding which characterized his life. And he gave in to the strangely liberating vortex of emotions produced by the attraction he felt for this man. Basilio and Hermilo began a secret love affair.

But Basilio could not be entirely happy; he also knew true happiness is reserved for only a few (very few) of the fortunate individuals in the world who are free of the extenuating circumstances that create insurmountable obstacles in their quest for happiness, and therefore freedom. He had great responsibilities that would not be easy to break away from.

Then the bittersweet experience of being caught in this clandestine affair happened. Carlos saw Basilio and Hermilo as they were bidding farewell to each other one day. Needless to say, Carlos, a perceptive yet devious man, a rich boy without the intelligence or wherewithal to make it on his own, realized instantly what was going on and seemed almost overjoyed as he beat up Basilio. He had followed him and as Basilio was about to open the door to his house, Carlos fell upon him with all the fury and violence the quasi-Neandertal was capable of.

Basilio spent nearly a month in the hospital recovering from his injuries. By then, Carlos had revealed to everyone Basilio's alter life in an overly enthusiastic way, and without ever implicating himself. "A robber," he had said. Basilio, the benevolent and sensitive man he was, had asked Hermilo, who was infuriated and quite capable of doing harm to Carlos, to not retaliate against his brother-in-law. He simply did not want Adela, out of the sincere affection he felt for her, to suffer twice; the loss of her husband and potential loss of her brother whom, despite his misgivings, she loved.

"Since, technically, I was not the true owner of Tiendas Benjamín, I did not continue to manage the company after the separation and divorce. Adela hired an accountant friend of ours to go on with the administration of the stores, and thankfully, they continued to prosper."

"Carlos, on the other hand," continued Basilio, "went into a downward spiral, becoming a notorious drunk, and eventually, Adela asked him to no longer be involved with the company."

"She has continued to give him a share of the profits, as per an arrangement to keep him away, but mainly because she cannot completely cut him out of what is rightfully his, whether he has any appreciation for it or not, or for the bigheartedness of his sister."

"Hermilo and I have been together since and opened up a business: 'Gimnasio Hércules.' He had always dreamed of having his own place," Basilio said.

"So, you see, amigos, tonight I got off easy with just a boxer's punch to the face. That is not to say that I don't live in constant fear of running into Carlos. I have often thought of leaving and starting all over again elsewhere. But that would be the coward's way out; in life, everyone must live with the consequences of what they have done. Happiness has once again eluded me, but I am conscious of and resigned to the fact that it is what I deserve, and until I die, it shall be so."

Marco sat back and absorbed Basilio's words and searched within his soul to find out how they applied to him.

But he was now feeling extremely tired, and as he closed his eyes and rested his head against the backrest, he could feel the silence that ensued after Basilio's story take him to a place of prolonged yearning, a place he had been many times without even knowing it. But he was so tired that he could no longer wrestle, struggle with his feelings at this point and he fell asleep for the third time that day as the van swayed this way and that in its path through the winding road, almost like a boat upon the waves of an endless sea of uncertainty.

11

Marco felt as if he had slept several hours, when in reality it had only been about thirty minutes. His head shook with the jostling of the van as José brought it to a stop at a lookout on the summit of the mountains, and again he woke with his head leaning against the window. And for two seconds after waking, he had no idea where he was; outside, silver light was shining all around, illuminating objects near and far in a mysterious way that was perplexing but strangely soothing. Was he in a spaceship that had just landed on some remote planet? *Strange, it had a moon so similar to the Earth's,* he thought. Then the side door slid open, the interior light came on, and everyone began to get out.

The view from the edge was impressive as they stood at the railing in silence. They were so high up and the moon was so bright, they could see where the horizon met a purple sky; the hills and the nearby trees shone in a spectacular incandescence almost as if producing a light of their own. Marco struggled to recall if he had ever, in all his travels, seen a more beautiful place.

He also thought, as he stood there dumbstruck by the breathtaking scene, and standing once more shoulder to shoulder with these unusual companions for which he now felt more than the beginnings of friendship, how humans, despite their differences, despite enormous adversity that many times leads to conflict, all have one thing in common: they can be humbled by the beauty of the natural world.

Suddenly, he noticed something over to the left where a nearby trail broke through the forest. The silhouettes of men, some of which were on horseback, were becoming clearly visible as they made a turn to their right and marched towards the highway. José had noticed them too. So, he quietly said to them, attempting to not reveal his apprehension, that they best be on their way.

Two minutes later as the van had passed two or three curves, they came upon the site where these men were crossing the highway. They were clad in military garb and wore bandanas on their faces, covering their nose and mouth – they were armed!

José brought the van to a halt since they were blocking the way and summoning them to stop. Pedro turned to see what was going on and raised his eyebrows, opening his eyes wide. Without saying anything, he opened the door and rushed out before anyone had a chance to ask any questions.

"Who are they?" asked Marco.

"Guerrilleros, señor," said José.

"Fighters for the Zapatista National Liberation Army," added Pablo. "You've heard of them, yes?"

They all had. Even Rainer. This was a band of anti-establishment revolutionaries that had made headlines for their audacious defiance of the government in Chiapas. Billed by the press as Marxists, at first they had organized town meetings and protests. But after they had been targeted and had faced brutal repression, they had taken to the hills to initiate a clandestine guerrilla war under the leadership of a notorious intellectual known only as Subcomandante Eugenio. Poorly equipped and outmanned always, and with only the support of the poorest citizens, they were not expected to get very far in their struggle.

Everyone now watched Pedro, illuminated brightly by the headlights, walk up to a tall man that had dismounted and had pulled down his bandana to reveal his face. He was cradling – more than pointing at anything in particular – a semiautomatic weapon. He was impressive as he stood soldier-like, back completely straight, stripes on his lapels, fierce in his countenance, holding his head high. He was a figure of undeniable charisma. *No wonder men follow him into battle,* thought Marco. The man greeted Pedro with a cautious handshake. They spoke for a while with an abundance of hand gestures that were impossible to read. Then he embraced Pedro. They were both smiling.

Once Pedro had returned to his seat, José put the van into gear and moved slowly forward as the men outside parted to let them pass. The impressive man, now back on his horse, saluted them briefly as he turned to leave into the darkness of the forest.

"That is Eugenio Alcázar," said Pedro. "We are good friends. And I used be a soldier in his army."

12

Pedro Nucamendi and Eugenio Alcázar had been inseparable classmates and best friends at the university in Mexico City. They had in common that they came from families that owned businesses requiring their help, and for this reason, they were studying business administration. At first, they also participated in sports and partied, but they had an incongruously sensitive, artistic side that led them to hang out with the cultured, intellectual, and opinionated crowd one finds in big city universities. So, Eugenio, through the influence of this group of friends, had taken electives in philosophy that shaped his life in a different way; he became an idealist and changed his major to political sciences.

More than anything, it was because of the writings of Karl Marx, Engels, and Lenin, and his observation of class struggle and the lack of social justice, that he embraced a socialist ideology. He vowed that someday, he would end oppression, exploitation, ignorance and poverty.

So, Eugenio organized a reading group to analyze the works of many of these great thinkers: Trotsky, Childe, Guesde, Ravdonikas, and the inevitable, Ché Guevara. Pedro attended sporadically and agreed with what was said at those meetings, but also realized where they were headed, that apparently harmless talking would eventually lead to indoctrination and political action, so he decided to stay away. But mainly, Pedro feared disappointing his parents who were sacrificing much to give him his education.

Slowly, Eugenio evolved into an outspoken activist, and because of his innate ability to lead, many followed him into the streets in his quest for social and moral equality. He organized worker's strikes, sit-downs in front of congress, human chains in front of police brigades, and other outrageous acts. He had progressed from activism to militancy and had many encounters with the law and was in an out of jail. He was a marked man. But he was also a prolific writer, not rehashing the old authors, but expounding on truly original ideas. Slowly, he had also evolved into the critical thinker, the badly needed ideologue for the working class of Mexico.

After graduation, when Pedro was ready to return to Chiapas, he searched for Eugenio; he wanted to say goodbye to the friend for whom he still had great affection, but he never found him. It was rumored he had gone into hiding. From a sanctuary somewhere, he would continue to write. His books would appear once in a while in newspaper and magazine stands.

"I always buy a copy when I come across one," Pedro said. "Titles such as: *The Children of Kulkulkán* or *The Vanishing Lands: A Treatise on the Decimation of the Mayan People and Their Homeland.*"

"That is why I had always suspected he was hiding here in Chiapas."

Then one day, everything changed for Pedro. Eugenio walked into the restaurant with three other men and sat near a window. They were constantly watching the people and cars passing by as Pedro observed them behind the counter across the room. He finally recognized Eugenio, who looked very thin, and greeted him with great emotion.

"Mi amigo, how good to see you," said Eugenio with genuine enthusiasm as he returned his old friend's embrace, tapping his back heartily.

They talked for several hours over lunch, had many beers, reminisced about old times, recreated the lost mystique of their student days.

And then it happened: Eugenio asked Pedro to join their cause. They were in the throes of a dangerous guerrilla war. "Think about it," he had said and gave him directions to a secret rendezvous point deep in the forest where he would be met and escorted to their center of operations. They had been able to acquire a great deal of weapons and medical supplies, the latter being an unavoidable, albeit tragic, necessity in war.

"Two days later, I was on my way," said Pedro. "The restaurant was now prospering, as I had mentioned, and in the hands of my very capable brother, Pablo." He went on to say, as if in deep contemplation, "There are things in life that you are meant to do. Once you've defined them but don't do them at the moment the opportunity arises, you shall regret it always. The desperate feeling of longing persists. Then suddenly, you are given a second chance to live by your principles, so you must take it. And that is what I did."

So, Pedro found himself fighting battles through the mountain passes in the outskirts of Yajalón, the corridors in the forests of Comitán, the flatlands near the waters of La

Angostura Dam. It seemed they were always outgunned, outmanned, and forever on the run. But they were unrelenting, no matter what the cost, never losing touch with the noble cause of bringing equality and justice to people who, in modern times, had never known either.

"Then, somehow, Pablo got word to me that our father had died. A longtime smoker, he had developed the lung cancer that took his life rather quickly. The pain was more than I could bear; the idea of losing that kind, hardworking man who had done so much for me. So, I came home."

Rainer broke the silence that followed Pedro's story and said, "Perhaps it is for the best. Your cause seems to be futile, if I may say so. From West Germany, we have seen what has happened to the other Germany in the East. Fortunately, for our brothers on that side, the Berlin Wall has fallen, just two weeks ago, as a matter of fact, and we hope to reunite the two Germanys soon because we know firsthand, after more than forty years of watching, that communism as a political, social and economic experiment has failed."

Rainer continued, "Look, I, too, have read Marx and Engels. On paper, socialism is beautiful, but utopian when it says that society does not consist of individuals. And it fails as much as capitalism to guarantee and sustain the living standards of the population. Under both systems, there have always been those that have too much and those that have too little. So, I guess it boils down to which system is better at guaranteeing personal freedom."

"Everything you're saying, Rainer, is true," Pedro conceded. "But our fight is no longer about orthodox Marxist theory, or moral and intellectual superiority. Class struggle in our particular scenario is about redeeming ourselves with the most forgotten and most deserving sector of society." He went on, "I'm referring to our indigenous people who have been marginalized and isolated within the lands of their ancestors and in which they can no longer prosper. All we are fighting for is recognition of their rights, love for their traditions, and respect for their humanity."

Pedro sighed wistfully. "That is the reason I joined Eugenio's army. So, you see, as Eugenio states in his latest book, the fight must go on."

13

As the ride continued, they were overcome by fatigue. By the time they reached San Cristóbal de las Casas, all were asleep, as José devotedly and expertly, like the captain of a ship, guided the vehicle through the imposing night, downward past the hills, towards the plains on the outskirts of Tuxtla Gutiérrez.

Upon entering the city limits, the shaking of the van and the glimmering streetlights woke the passengers one by one. And for two seconds after waking, Marco thought he was on Zaragoza Avenue, the ludicrous Eastern gateway into Mexico City. He was surprised at how little traffic there was, because even at 10 o'clock at night, the streets should have been bustling with cars. Then he remembered, he was in Chiapas and this must be Tuxtla Gutiérrez.

They each gave José directions to where they were going as they exchanged business cards and telephone numbers, vowing to see each other again. Marco was the last one to be dropped off and he felt a bit lonely as he and José proceeded in total silence.

Pablo, Pedro, Basilio and Pánfilo were all now at home, and Rainer was at a small bed and breakfast near the center of town. Finally, Marco reached his destination, the Hotel Grijalba, with a sigh of relief.

Once he had checked into his room, he showered, put on his pajamas, and got into bed, where he melted into the crisp, cool sheets, a sensation that overwhelmed him; he had intended on reading his speech one more time, but he gave way to the glorious feeling of being in a soft bed, in a room with a pleasant table light, a gentle breeze blowing through the open window, while recalling the invigorating events of the day. He quickly fell into a deep sleep.

14

The following morning, Marco gave his presentation to a packed crowd in a grand conference room downstairs and it was met with much acclaim and myriad questions from an endless assortment of people from all over Mexico and South America, many of them young and thirsting for knowledge.

As gratifying as that was, when he recalled his thoughts and the events from the day before, he felt, all over again, oppression in his heart. So, after the obligatory chatting with the attendees of the meeting during that evening's cocktail party (*the cubas he ordered weren't as good as Pablo's,* he thought), he excused himself. But instead of going up to his room, he took a taxi to the Restaurant Las Brasas.

When he arrived, the other five were already assembled there; it had been as if they all knew that this was the logical place where they would meet again. He was greeted with the effusiveness with which one greets an old friend, which was odd but comforting. Despite the brief time they knew each other, the friendship had been sealed.

They talked and laughed and continued their conversations, picking up where they had left off. It was a pleasant evening; the food was good, the drinks soothing, and the company fraternal.

The next day, Marco had breakfast with Rainer at his little hostel before going their separate ways. Rainer took a bus further south, past the Chichonal Volcano to Tapachula and into Guatemala to find passage back to the United States and eventually, Europe. Marco was now able to get a direct flight back to Mexico City.

It was dark by the time he retrieved his car and drove across the city to his home in the southern suburbs, all the time hoping, wishing that Belina had changed her mind and that she would be waiting up for him with a pot of coffee, or a glass of wine. He really needed to tell her that he felt he was a changed man. But it was not to be. True to her word, she had left their home, this gesture, a final, opprobrious statement that their marriage had ended. On the kitchen counter laid a note with a sad, unfortunate message that read:

Dear Marco,

I'm sorry about how things have turned out. I truly wish that it could have been different and that we had found a better solution, but I can no longer go on pretending. We must, of course, keep in touch for the sake of the boys and come to a suitable arrangement.

(It was signed, ironically,)

Love, Belina.

Marco didn't know if he was more bothered by the finality that it implied or by the lack of imagination in her words. He thought the note was annoyingly conventional. Despite everything, did he not deserve more?

He rested his head on the kitchen counter and thought of the amazing journey with his newfound friends that somehow, strangely, had given him a sense of freedom, maybe even a new outlook on life. Nevertheless, as he got ready for bed, he felt as if a pressure valve inside him had burst and he did something he couldn't recall ever having done in all his adult life, he cried himself to sleep.

15

They say that time heals all suffering and that we can become accustomed to anything, even chronic pain or unimaginable adversity. But six months had now passed since Belina had abandoned their home and Marco saw how little progress he had made. Marco realized that Rainer had been right in saying that totally immersing himself in his work wasn't going to make him feel any better about his situation or himself. Worse, it seemed he was no longer interested in his work; he no longer found any meaning in answering the profound questions that arose in that small, particular field of science he had chosen to be in and could no longer meet head on, or even tangentially, the intellectual challenges it required. In other words, he was no longer happy doing what he did.

It was amazing how the shattering of his personal life had created an avalanche of emotions that had covered and smothered him for good. Marco knew he needed a change; it was time to reinvent himself, as they say. So, he took his sabbatical year at the university and moved to Tuxtla Gutiérrez.

He began his clinical work at the General Hospital with a renewed sense of purpose, putting in many more than the required hours, seeing patients from all walks of life, but mainly the poor and downtrodden, finding tremendous and unexpected joy in it. He cured skin diseases, treated malnourished children, cared for expectant mothers, attended to the chronically ill, and resolved emergencies. He counseled families, shared the sadness with those who had lost loved ones, even shedding tears with them. He was suddenly in that other realm of life he had forgotten about, facing now, head on, that other face of medicine, and he felt like an artist. He no longer worried about placing his attention entirely on an isolated biological phenomenon in a controlled setting with few variables. He no longer cared about it, because that practice had only afforded him a minuscule part of the answer that by itself was meaningless unless it was viewed with all the other pieces of the puzzle, like grains of sand coming together to create the vision of a beach. Not that his research had served no purpose, on the contrary, it was the grain of sand that someone might need to create the big picture, so to speak, or at least a good chunk of it. It was just that now, here was the entire experiment of nature in each unique human being that walked, talked, suffered, was exposed to countless variables, and that represented an almost impossible amount of data to analyze.

Marco never suspected how easily he would regain his clinical skills, like riding a bike, he told himself, as he lay in bed on lonely, sleepless nights. And now the 'Eureka' moment was about the discovery of himself; it was like fast, downhill ride on rocky trails, with jumps and dips, wind and sand in his face, heart beating in time to the excitement… He had recovered the long dormant thrill, the romance, the mystique of what it meant to be doctor.

Marco was also surprised that he began to have luck with the ladies. He was not a handsome man, but still not unpleasant to look at, and it seemed what attracted them the most was his air of confidence, whether real or not, an arrogance afforded to him by his great intellect. There was Mari Toña, the pretty, flighty one who almost immediately wanted to marry him. Angelita was the curvaceous secretary that had seduced him in a burst of true and never before known passion in the bathroom of his office. Marvelous, intelligent Vicky, the speech pathologist who could talk about Piaget and child development; she had taught him, as they watched the fireworks at a nearby church through the window of her apartment, the true art of lovemaking. Then there was Esther, the brainy, brown-haired, beautiful social worker who drank Scotch whiskey and talked about social justice as they watched the moon dip into the ocean on the beaches of Tonalá.

He realized he had become what Milan Kundera defines as an 'epic' lover, always searching for, and feeling satisfied in finding, that one-millionth part in each woman that made her different from the rest. Ironically, he (Kundera would be distressed to know this) was also a 'lyrical' lover, always searching as well for the ideal woman. Here he always felt frustrated because, no matter how tender the kiss, how warm the embrace, how erotic the touch of a new body, no matter how much pleasure he derived from each encounter, he could never stop comparing his new lovers to Belina.

His work also had its damper. He discovered that the behavior of the hospital administrators was less than ethical and noticed how funds were being discreetly funneled into private bank accounts. By God, the director was building himself a new house in an upscale neighborhood while the hospital was in disrepair and nearly crumbling, running on the bare minimum of equipment and personnel, much to the detriment of the patients, the very people they were there to serve!

"What are we?" he asked his friends Pánfilo and Basilio, one day when they had met for coffee. "What have we become when greed overrides what is morally correct?"

"It has always been so, *amigo*," Basilio replied lamely, because he didn't know what else to say. "Around here, we are used to a government that takes and takes and never gives back. Sadly, it is part of our way of life. At least we have our family and our friends to give meaning to our lives. So, *salud amigo*, to friendship," he said, as he raised his coffee cup in a mock toast.

Marco remembered the moment in the van when Basilio had toasted to friendship…and to recapturing lost love. At that precise moment of confusion and renewed angst, he wished he had one of Pablo's cubas in his hand instead of coffee.

16

It was Marco's day off and he wanted to sleep but was awakened by the sound of loud music emanating from the vecindad across the street. There seemed to be some sort of festivity, a birthday perhaps or the celebration for a quinceañera, he really didn't know but in the two seconds after opening his eyes, he thought he was back in the Parrilla Norteña restaurant in Teapa sharing food and drinks with his five friends while listening to Pánfilo tell the story of his life. Then he realized he was at home in bed, sweating, the fan doing nothing to quell the midday heat.

But today was a special day. It was the anniversary of the journey of the six and there was going to be a reunion at Las Brasas.

Like the year before, by the time he arrived, the others were already there, except for Pedro. Rainer had surprised everyone by making the trip all the way from Germany and had been met with vigorous, back-slapping embraces. Once again, the conversations began.

Interesting changes had occurred in each of their lives in those twelve months.

Pablo was now married to Erica, a petite, pretty girl with hazel eyes. She was helping Pablo's mother with the restaurant. Erica and Pablo would exchange occasional, loving glances and Marco thought that the quiet, enigmatic Pablo was probably, in this particular moment, the happiest man in the world. He had not sought change and had remained secure in the safety his family provided and had prospered and found love.

Pedro on the other hand, had been gone for the past two months. He had rejoined the struggle with his long-time friend, Eugenio. For him, everything was about change, or rather creating change, especially for those who were oppressed. So he was back in the sierra ignoring the hardships that this implied. Perhaps that is what gave meaning to his life, the unexpected occurring every day, always renewing the panorama of his life.

Pánfilo announced that he had finally been able to open up a brand new Libros Matera bookstore in Villahermosa with his brother, Raymundo. He would often go there to do book reviews and give suggestions to teachers, much as he did in Tuxtla Gutiérrez; the 'Bookman' had become an erudite. For this reason, he had been offered associate professorships at the universities of both locales.

Marco talked to them about his divorce but on a brighter note also about his revitalized interest and new vision in medicine and how this had afforded him a semblance of happiness. Pánfilo told him he would talk to the people at the university to see about a teaching position at the medical school.

"I'd like that very much," Marco said.

Basilio and Hermilo were still together and Gimnasio Hércules had become very profitable. He and Adela had become close friends once more. He was back at helping her manage the stores. Carlos, her brother, had met a tragic end; in his philandering, he had become involved with drug traffickers.

"But he was probably incompetent even in that. No one knows the exact details, but he had been strangled and his body was found on the side of the highway," Basilio told them.

Rainer and Dora, sadly, never got back together. He had decided to leave the prosecutor's office in München and was now a lawyer for the Umweltbundesamt, Germany's environmental protection agency.

Ever the poet, Rainer stated, "I was tired of the sad business of putting people in jail. In this past year, I have become acutely aware of the need to protect nature. It is our responsibility since we humans are her gifted children. I figured this would be a much happier endeavor, to protect the forests I love so much, as well as all the living beings that make it their home and in so doing, we are ensuring our own well-being."

Marco glanced at his watch and realized it was nearly 10:00 PM. He was having such a good time that he had forgotten about the meeting for hospital department heads which was to take place at the State Secretary of Health Office. After he had said good-bye to everyone, Pablo met him at the door and handed him a small package wrapped in brown paper.

Marco could feel it was a book and could almost guess who the author was, probably the latest book by Eugenio Alcázar, he figured.

"Pedro asked me to give you this," he said. "You will find something there for you on a page he marked."

"Thank you, Pablo. I promise to read it," Marco said sincerely.

17

Dr. Miguel Ángel Morales Best, the Secretary of Health, was a hardnosed politician and frowned on unpunctuality. But more than that, he detested being contradicted and ran his office in tyrannical fashion. Though he inconvenienced everyone, he always held his meetings late at night. It was also well-known that, because of his close ties with the Governor, who was also his brother-in-law, he would fire people for challenging his authority.

For this reason, Marco hated these meetings; they were characterized by ludicrous kowtowing to this obnoxious man that Marco saw as a caricature of a dictator.

Marco entered the conference room late and was met with intense staring. Unfortunately, he was also drunk.

As he took his seat, he heard them talking already about the budget for the next fiscal year. "Absurd," he murmured to himself. *Since when,* he thought, *did any of this talking ever accomplish anything. When have they ever had what was really needed to better serve the people? All they are worried about,* he mused, *are their own pockets. What a bunch of self-serving, inhumane hypocrites;* he thought this almost out loud.

What made it more unbearable were the surroundings. This office and conference room were luxuriously furnished, brightly and cozily lighted, beautiful artwork was on the walls. But what tipped the balance and turned his inconformity into militancy was the fact that it was air-conditioned, a comfort not enjoyed by the patients.

They were now looking at him. It was his turn to speak. The only one concerned that Marco appeared to be perturbed while lost in his thoughts was his friend, Iván, the vascular surgeon. He knew what was on Marco's mind. They had talked many times at lunchtime about the very things Marco found inexcusable, and he agreed. But there was, in Iván's way of thinking, as in Basilio's, little they could do to change things.

Marco had lost all his inhibitions, as he looked straight at the Secretary of Health, the most powerful man in medicine in the entire state, and said, trying not to slur his words, "I think we should all be ashamed of ourselves." He paused trying to find the right words, then went on. "Look around you. Why should you, Mr. Secretary, have the luxury of air-conditioning when our patients do not? They are ill and we must provide for their comfort as part of the healing process. But their rooms are hot and inhospitable, sometimes without even sheets on the beds."

Everyone looked appalled except Iván, who was struggling to suppress a smile. But Marco had not finished.

"All I see, to be perfectly honest, is pilfering." This was hitting home but was putting them all on the defensive. "Where does all the money go? We have a sizeable allotment from the federal government, so why have we never replaced the rusty X-ray machine, the outdated EKG machines, the malfunctioning lab instruments, or modernized the pharmacy." Still, he went on. "Like I said, we are all guilty and should be ashamed that we cannot be better at what we do. I can no longer be party to this mockery."

Marco stormed out of the room before anybody could reply, nearly tripping as he hurriedly made his way to the door. He could hear rumbling behind him and guessed that the meeting was over. He made his way quickly to a large balcony on the third floor where there was a view of the mountains. He needed to clear his mind.

There was a warm, soothing breeze; the moonlight was subtle but definite. He closed his eyes and for two seconds, he imagined he was standing at the look out where he and his friends had stood a year ago, when they were halfway into their journey. Marco felt the same pang of foreboding as he looked out at the majestic landscape. He was again, he thought, a broken man, but now also a marked man. He knew his newly found happiness, or the illusion of it, had been too good to be true.

Suddenly, Marco was aware of someone standing next to him. He was a big man with all the appearances of a thug.

"Mr. Secretary says to tell you that he accepts your resignation. And *I* am telling you that around these parts, people have disappeared for saying even less than what you just said to him." The thug was snarling.

Marco didn't know where he was getting the courage but he turned to face him and replied emphatically. "What are you going to do, shoot me? Well, the bullets shall find their path as if they already knew the way, for I feel I am dying already. But I find comfort in saying that my conscience is clear. How about yours?"

The man seemed startled at Marco’s daring words and backed off without saying anything, vanishing as stealthily as he had come, back into the shadows.

18

It was after midnight by the time Marco made it home. He turned on all the lights, as he checked every room making sure no one was hiding in his apartment. This sudden paranoia seemed justified; he had not appreciated the words of the big man on the balcony and he was now, for the first time, feeling afraid.

Perhaps nothing would come of it, he tried telling himself, feeling a little more rational after he had poured himself a glass of wine. Anyway, the damage had been done. His career was pretty much over; word would get around through those endless circles of gossip, would even get back to the university department heads. They would know how he had shown up intoxicated to an important meeting and in a drunken outburst had insulted the state's Secretary of Health and all those in attendance. His words were tantamount to calling them corrupt and immoral, things politicians hate to hear and to which they react harshly. It didn't matter one bit that he was actually telling the truth. What mattered was that Marco had violated an absurd unwritten law that protects those that violate moral truths; don't make waves, they say, lest you be the next one to be thrown overboard. It was a dishonest world and

Marco, in his fairly recent professional and emotional rebirth, so to speak, had had enough.

"What now?" he muttered to himself. He sat back and closed his eyes but in two seconds, the image of Pablo handing him Pedro's gift popped into his head. Once he had unwrapped the book, he was surprised to see that it was not written by Eugenio as he had suspected; it was a volume of the collected poems of Konstantino Kavafis, a poet he knew Pedro admired. He opened it to a dog-eared page and began reading:

Progress is a tremendous edifice – all of us carry our stone;
someone brings words, someone advice, another documents
– Day to day, the tower grows taller.

But a hurricane, a furious wind
approaches, the honest workers hurry
to defend their frustrated labor.
And everything is lost; every life is spent
suffering abuse and pain, for a future generation

that we would ask be honest, happy,
with a long life, rich in wisdom,
without hard or servile toil.

Meanwhile, this generation never, never lives.
Its work shall be ruined
and its vain efforts shall begin anew.

Marco knew exactly what Pedro was trying to tell him; these words expressed with beauty and eloquence the principles by which Pedro ruled his life and that Marco had acquired slowly, insensibly. He had become an idealist.

He flipped through the pages and came across a piece of paper with what appeared to be a map and instructions in Pedro's handwriting on how to reach the rendezvous point where he would be met and taken to their base of operations deep in the forest, an unnamed place somewhere in the vicinity of San Cristobal de las Casas.

Marco now knew what he had to do.

The following morning, he packed some things into a backpack and began the next part of what now seemed an interminable journey, one with a twisting path and a revolving door.

19

Marco was now in uniform: some old fatigues that seemed to be stolen from a surplus warehouse somewhere. He was jostling back and forth as the truck, an old, open, medium-sized farm truck converted into some sort of military vehicle, headed into the hills on a bouncy, dirt road. The truck was followed by a poorly equipped, rag-tag army; some were armed with shotguns or hunting rifles, others with machetes, and still others without any weapons at all – they had believed their presence created the illusion of a larger, fighting force. Subcommander Eugenio Alcázar was sitting next to him and seriously babbling on about something, but Marco only pretended to pay attention, his mind was racing on elsewhere.

During the two weeks that had elapsed after abandoning Tuxtla Gutiérrez, making his way to the rendezvous point followed by a short basic training, Marco kept reminding himself, as he sat by the campfire each night, about the things that motivate radical actions. He was actually going off to war; this thought made him feel both terrified and exhilarated and the anticipation of it was almost unbearable. Can anyone ever be prepared for it? The truth was, he didn't really know why he was there and felt scared at how easily he had embraced a cause that made men capable of risking their lives to defend it.

Marco thought about how his life had changed over the past year; thought of how he had changed. Once again, he was experiencing that bittersweet confusion that now seemed to characterize his life, when before it had always been methodical, structured to the point of obsessiveness. And he had also been massively selfish and ambitious, thinking only of advancing his career. This had caused him to lose his wife, had made his children despise him.

But on the day the six friends ventured over the mountain, through the deep, deep forest, he had begun to feel free for the first time in his life. And he realized that the obstinate constancy of his former, prearranged life had been out of fear of straying from his comfort zone, out of a dreadful fear of change. But true change had begun on that fateful day. It was the first chip off the concrete wall he had constructed around himself, a wall that eventually ceased to exist despite his losses, despite the fact that he was going off to war. Now he didn't know what would happen next, but he felt free in his pursuit to find out.

The convoy moved into a clearing that was well hidden from the road to form a new base camp. It would be dark soon but when they finally settled in, he began to feel comfortable, as he took in the sights and sounds of this beautiful place. Above the tall trees, the sky was pink; some clouds hung overhead, moving as slowly as the Earth, Marco thought, lumbering off to nowhere in particular. A flock of green parrots passed rapidly, squawking, wings all aflutter. High above, an eagle floated as if on a sea of air, majestic in its wandering. There was a breeze that moved the air steadily, deliciously; it rustled the heavy foliage of the trees softly, in a rhythm that, with eyes closed, mimicked the sea. The footsteps of small animals could be heard moving the carpet of leaves, as they scurried off, oblivious to any impending doom. The baritone roar of an animal identified by one of the soldiers as a jaguar was startling but exhilarating. The water of a nearby stream made a crackling, soothing sound as it rushed past. He went down to sit by its bank feeling at ease, feeling almost a peace as he had never experienced, he mused, and Marco wondered how long this feeling, this idyllic moment, could last. Based on what he had been through that year, he knew it could not last forever. Indeed, nothing ever does, he concluded.

Suddenly, gunfire erupted about a hundred yards away. The bullets hissed angrily, as they whizzed through the trees violently tearing off leaves and twigs that rained down on the men. Ten minutes later, Marco lay dying; one hand in the water, moisture running up his sleeve, his legs contorted where he fell, eyes open facing the sky, his other hand on his chest over a growing bloodstain where a bullet had entered his chest. He was struggling to breathe.

The government could no longer put up with the rebellion and had infiltrated their ranks with spies. This unlikely band of untrained, unsophisticated fighters had become, nonetheless, a formidable threat to the status quo; thus, this final, brutal offensive against them.

20

They say that when you are dying, your life parades instantaneously and uncontrollably before you in flashbacks. This happened to Marco, who was well-aware that he had been mortally wounded.

Marco was twelve-years-old and saw himself with his two brothers on a city bus. They donned their baseball uniforms and were returning from the Olmeca Little League field, laughing, joyous: Marco had hit a game-winning homerun that day.

His mother appeared before him, greeting him with a hug and kiss, promising to make him his favorite dessert: Milk and rice pudding, sweetened with cajeta and sprinkled with cinnamon – he had made the honor roll.

His father stood behind her, smiling. He was a caring man who had inspired his son to achieve great things.

His mentor, Dr. Cordoba, now stood next to Marco, content that his star pupil was shaking hands with the University Rector as he received his first award.

Then he saw Marquito and Mario, their curly, reddish hair blowing in the breeze. They smiled at him; he noticed Mario was missing a tooth.

Belina! She appeared in front of his eyes enveloped in a tenuous mist. She looked young and beautiful, just as he remembered her on the day they met, wearing the black skirt that flattered her hips and the white blouse that revealed her youthful skin. She was smiling more enticingly than the Mona Lisa. Her eyes sparkled, beckoning him, lovingly, he thought, to a rendezvous of love! Marco knew at that moment – finally – that she was the woman he had loved most in his life.

And in the two seconds before closing his eyes forever, Marco Rosen, for the first time in his life, felt truly happy.

Moonlight in the Lost Lands

"Love begins at the point when a woman enters
her first word into your poetic memory."
– Milan Kundera

Nearly a year had passed since I last saw her. When we drove out of Sofia that day, I lay stupidly in the back seat of the van, bleeding from my left nostril, my upper lip swollen to three times its normal size; I was dizzy, and feeling ashamed.

They had rescued me and forced me to go to avoid anything worse happening to me. But now, I was back, on my own, and in hopeless despair. I needed to find her but knew the odds of that happening were close to nothing. Still, I had to try, had to know she was alright, safe, or, at least, the same.

I knocked twice on the door of the apartment we shared for that one night; I refused to let that night die, refused to let time whittle it away into endless, absurd fragments until nothing remained but the sensation of a memory. The apartment building still needed repair, her apartment door was still cracked and chipping. Standing there, I suddenly experienced the burden of unrelenting time. After knocking for a third time, the door opened just a crack but enough for me to see it was not her. It was an older woman. A strange woman, who seemed appalled at the sight of me, at the scruffiness I had acquired after almost two years on the road: A beard, long oily hair, dirty clothes, a tired look. She had reason to be wary; here was this odd vision of a man, who barely spoke any Bulgarian, inquiring about someone she didn't even know.

When I last saw Nevena, she was already leaving for work, a travel bag in her hand; we were going to meet later, and run away together; perhaps in Istanbul we could find work and eventually passage to the West. But she never showed up.

At the motor club where she worked, and where we had met, they told me nobody knew her; in fact, everyone, they said, was new to the office. But there was one girl I had seen before leaving Sofia. I pleaded with her to tell me more, wondered if there was anyone to contact or if there was any way to find her, but she refused to speak out.

I had now wandered through the timeless streets of Sofia for two months, aimlessly hoping for a gift from the magic hand of chance, a fortunate, improbable encounter. So I wandered. I rode all the trolley car lines, walked through all the parks, visited all the markets, lingered in all the old churches. I hesitated every time I saw a girl with shiny, brown hair, scurrying off in a winter coat and woolen cap. My heart would race, but it was always the same result. It was not her.

***

1

I was the first to see the rundown guardhouse and the gate with the faded, red and white stripes. We had reached the border rather quickly after leaving Pirot in eastern Serbia. Our goal for that day was the ancient city of Sofia.

We would soon be leaving Yugoslavia. The year was 1970 and it was the dead of winter. We had already traveled the entire length of Europe in a southeasterly direction, and only one country, Bulgaria, remained before reaching Turkey where Istanbul, that majestic, millennial crossroads, awaited to usher us into Asia. Our ultimate goal was India.

I met them on the ferry ride between Dover and Oostende. I was alone and trying unsuccessfully to avoid feeling seasick as I stared out at the roiling waters of the foggy English Channel. Suddenly, there they were, on a bench across from me, introducing themselves. The first to speak was Manjeet, the brainy one and with whom I would develop a good friendship. Kumar, definitely the boss, spoke next, snatching away the conversation in an endless discourse. The other two were Balbir, a jolly, gentle giant, and the improbably named, Paul Herr, the quiet, handsome one.

They were London filmmakers commissioned with a documentary about travel to India, their homeland, and they had decided to experience it firsthand. So they loaded up their old but well-maintained English Ford van with all the necessities and set off for the long-awaited adventure, full of expectations, with maps and an itinerary from the British Motor Club in hand.

During the ferry crossing, I negotiated with them a ride to Brussels. But I had been a patient listener to the details of their quest, so, upon disembarking the ferry, Manjeet asked me if I would care to travel with them to India. True to my freewheeling spirit and endowed with an incurable wanderlust (that had guided me to take time off from school to 'see the world'), I accepted without hesitation.

We had our share of setbacks along the way: We argued with a Belgian gas station attendant over his attempt to overcharge us; we had been become helplessly lost in the traffic of Frankfurt; we were snowbound in the Austrian Alps, and, just west of Belgrade, we had trouble with a faulty carburetor whose replacement had to be shipped from Germany.

And now, upon reaching the Bulgarian border outpost at Kalotina, armed guards were ordering us to stop!

2

The border crossing took longer than expected. Being the only American in the group, my passport was scrutinized thoroughly. The official showed it around, everyone nodding, seemingly amused. He then walked towards me.

"Alberto Madariaga?" The official held my passport up and was reading my name, looking back and forth from my picture to me, a quizzical look on his face.

"That is a rather unusual name for an American," he finally said.

I had heard that before and was tiring of it. What is a 'usual' name for an American anyway? I guess people stereotype Americans as Anglos. But immigrants flock from everywhere imaginable, so in America, any name is possible. I did not want to explain again, to him or anybody else, that I am a first generation American whose parents were from Mexico. So I nodded in agreement, but said nothing.

Annoyed that no explanation on my part was forthcoming, he pounded his rubber stamp on a blank page in my passport, smudging the ink, closed it, and handed it back without addressing me further. As he walked away, he muttered something to the others in a low voice. The only word I understood clearly was 'hippie.' Another stereotype for an American, I mused.

He had given me a transit visa for five days only. Nevertheless, we reasoned it would be more than enough time to cross Bulgaria to the Turkish border. But one of the van's tires was slowly deflating, and had begun to wear unevenly making it dangerous to continue on the winding roads of the Balkans. Kumar looked up in his directory a possible affiliate of the motor club in Sofia and, amazingly, found it. Not knowing how long it would take to have the tire replaced, we decided it would be wise to spend the night in Sofia.

The early afternoon had turned gray and snow seemed imminent, but the ride was gratifying nonetheless. The sinuous road, dotted with villages lost in time, led us through hills of startling beauty. I remember thinking, sleepily, superficially dreaming, how an entire lifetime of traveling would not suffice to see all of the magnificence in the world, the grandeur of nature we are so keen on destroying. I wanted to see it all before it was changed forever. Mostly everyone in my generation felt the same way. Born in the post-war era, we had witnessed almost magical technological advances, but also rampant industrialization wreaking havoc on the environment in the name of 'big business,' euphemistically called progress: Ghastly urban pollution, the decimation of forests and wetlands; the unchecked rape of nature with no regard for its other living creatures. And we had also grown up in an era of cold war detente; of two major powers instilling an ever-present fear of nuclear annihilation, stockpiling their machines of death. But for now, there were splendors to be seen. So here I was, riding freely through this wondrous land.

3

A sudden movement of the van jolted me back to reality. We were entering Sofia, and the van was now limping through the narrow streets that were overrun by tiny vehicles and trolley cars. We passed grand, old buildings, majestic ancient churches. But, in alarming contrast, there were also many large, identical housing projects, and gray, seemingly abandoned buildings that appeared to serve no purpose whatsoever, the hallmark of Eastern Bloc, communist-era cities.

We located the motor club called 'Union des Automovilistes Bulgares' on Place Pozitano and found a place to park. By now, the bad tire had given up its loyal but exhausting effort and was nearly flat.

The motor club office was a large, nearly empty room except for a few desks with typewriters, catalog type books, and posters tacked on the wall. A coat rack stood stiffly in a corner, diligently holding a single winter coat and a scarf. A telephone lay on one of the desks, and sitting there was an attractive, young woman busy with some unknown task. She looked up as we wandered sheepishly over to her desk. We were relieved to discover that she spoke English and once we explained what we needed (and she had checked

Kumar's membership card), she pulled out a file and made some phone calls in wonderful sounding Bulgarian.

About fifteen minutes later, a mechanic showed up. He was a cheerful, burly man, with dirty fingernails – the universal sign of the working man. He greeted everyone heartily in broken English, shaking hands firmly one by one. Kumar and Paul followed him in the van to his shop while Manjeet, Balbir, and I remained in the office chatting amicably with the girl for quite some time, sipping delicious, hot tea sweetened with honey.

"Nevena," I blurted out during a lag in the conversation, surprising her.

She realized I was reading the nametag that was pinned to her blouse and she smiled warmly, rather amused, because it was written in Cyrillic letters. She asked me if I spoke Bulgarian and I said, no. But I went on to explain that I had gone through a recent phase of reading nothing but classic Russian literature and had attempted, unsuccessfully, to learn the language on my own through old Berlitz records.

"Don't laugh, but what I wanted was to read Dostoyevsky in the original Russian."

This, I eventually realized, had been too ambitious and unattainable from the start. But I did learn the alphabet well enough to read words, even when I didn't really even know what they meant.

This story seemed to please her immensely and it was then that she looked at me in a way I would never forget: Straight into my eyes with a disquieting gaze and a broad smile.

Mesmerized, I let myself observe her in a moment of near epiphany. Her eyelids puffed slightly as she smiled nearly hiding her light-brown eyes. Her chestnut hair was done in a ponytail but bangs fell coquettishly over her right eyebrow. And the mystery of her body, only insinuated by her loosely fitting blouse and skirt, was begging to be solved.

But it was that wonderfully alluring smile that had captivated me most. As it formed, a dimple appeared in each ample cheek, and as her full, pink lips, parted, slightly crooked front teeth were revealed. Enthralled by the image of her teeth, it occurred to me that it is the possibility for this sort of imperfections that makes someone all the more human and desirable. I thought of this much as Shakespeare might have as he wrote a tender sonnet about his own mistress's defects. Her eyes, he wrote, were 'nothing like the sun,' but her beauty still was 'as rare as any she belied with false compare.' In essence, Nevena needed no false compare, for she was beautiful even with, or especially because of, her imperfections. I figure no other way to describe her would do her justice as I remember her on that day of fading sunlight and honey tea.

Just then, Kumar and Paul entered triumphantly.

"All's well, my friends," Kumar asserted. "Now we must find a hotel and rest our weary bones," stating this emphatically, with a flare of drama, in that Indian/British accent I have always found to be strangely, but pleasingly, eloquent.

Nevena said, putting on her coat and scarf, she knew just the place, and it was just around the corner, small but comfortable. It had been rebuilt after the war to accommodate the influx of foreigners, especially Russian dignitaries. So, she assured us, there would be all the usual amenities to which we were accustomed.

"And it has a parking garage where your possessions shall be safe," she added.

After Nevena had given directions, Kumar, Balbir, and Paul boarded the van to drive to the hotel. Manjeet yelled out for them to wait, and whispered to me, the back of his hand shielding his words, "I think she fancies you." As he got into the van, he winked at me with abundant mischief in his eye.

4

So, Nevena and I lagged behind, shyly trying to prolong the moment in which we were suddenly alone. Had she felt the attraction too? It seemed we no longer knew what to say, and our animated conversation from before had fallen silent. But it was a comfortable silence, for we had reverted to an ancient language, brought down through the ages and spoken without words between a man and a woman. It was heightened by the overwhelming surroundings: the prolonged sunset – a star already visible, the churning air – cold and invigorating on our faces, the silhouettes of the building – rapidly growing their shadows, the stream of tiny cars – their claxons resounding comically.

I have always loved walking down city streets in search of the things that give them their own particular charm. Mexico City has its purposeful chaos; New York City its massive structures and endless hordes of people shuffling off to who-knows-where? Paris and London have their city lights glittering in their respective rivers. And Sofia has, I found, the mystical allure of centuries of history.

Or was the magic of the moment due to the fact that I was walking down this particular street, in this particular city, with this particular woman, someone I had just barely met, but for whom I felt, nonetheless, a compelling and inexplicable closeness? She was a woman, I imagined, with whom, in some long-gone era, I could have traveled arm in arm through an untamed wilderness or walked upon the sandy shore of an eons-old, shimmering sea.

As we passed a small café, we stopped to look through the big picture window. The ambience seemed cozy. The waiters wore black vests and bow ties. White tablecloths were in place, along with a single candle and a vase with a single rose. We found each other's gaze, allured like moths to its warm, inviting light.

"I am rather hungry. Perhaps we can meet here, in one hour, yes?" Nevena asked. "I must go freshen up," she added, almost apologetically.

She leaned into me and grabbing my arm whispered, "Be careful, we are being followed."

Then she walked away.

5

In the dwindling light, I hadn't noticed the man walking parallel to us across the street. But there he was, standing quite still and remarkably in keeping with the stereotype of a spy, or a secret agent from a television show. He was a big man, wearing a black trench coat, and incongruous sunglasses (it was now dark, after all) that didn't allow me to determine if he was looking my way. Feeling a little perturbed, I decided to walk on briskly towards the hotel.

Finding the room I was to share with Manjeet and Paul, I thought about my imminent, unexpected rendezvous with Nevena, and what a remarkable occurrence that was. I knew guys to whom it happened all the time. My friend, Andrés, was just that sort of charismatic man; tall, with dashing good looks. He could sit down at a bar, feigning indifference, and fifteen minutes later, a-la-Humphrey Bogart, have a woman walk up and ask him to light up her cigarette.

But I had never been so lucky, and felt nervous. I also felt embarrassed that after close inspection of my belongings, all stuffed randomly into my backpack, I had no suitable clothes to wear. Nonetheless, I showered rapidly (mainly because the hot water lasted about two minutes; so much for the usual amenities), and dressed with the least wrinkled clothes I had.

Now ready, I stomped out of the hotel hurriedly towards the café, hoping to arrive ahead of her.

But she was already waiting for me at the door.

I don't know if I was more agitated from having rushed off in almost intolerable anticipation, or from the stunning image she created as she waited there, still and alone, wearing her white woolen cap, her hair now loose to shoulder length, her face made up in gentle tones that accentuated her honey-colored eyes, and red lipstick, bright and sensuous. She wore the same navy-blue coat, and underneath it I could feel the definite curves of a woman as she greeted me with a tight hug and a firm, sticky kiss on the cheek that left the tenuous ghost of her lips on my face. The scent of lavender from her soft skin lingered stubbornly on my nostrils, and I breathed it in deeply.

As we entered the restaurant, I glanced back and saw Mr. Trench Coat again, sitting on a bench across the street. As cars passed, they momentarily illuminated his face, now with glasses removed, though his features remained as indefinable as before.

We found a table fairly quickly despite the crowd and as we ate the meal she selected of funny-sounding things like 'shopska' salad and 'spanachena' soup, we drank Melnik wine.

"Rumor has it that this was Winston Churchill's favorite red wine," she stated.

For some inexplicable reason, this created levity and she lifted her glass to toast the brilliant, old statesman who had led his nation through war and crises. I realized that she knew more about my world than I of hers. We were from two disparate halves of the world, knowing about each other only through what political propagandists would allow us. So, the more she spoke, the more attractive she became, precisely because of this intelligence that made her able to breach geographical differences and the absurd boundaries of politics. And she was cultured beyond her years. Definitely a reader, she was knowledgeable of even American writers; Steinbeck, Hemmingway, Wilder. It was now I who was immensely pleased.

I also learned she was a widow. While in her second year as an art major at the university, she met Petar, who was ready to enter law school, and they fell in love. But after the Prague Spring of 1968, Bulgaria had become more strongly aligned with the Soviet Union, so there followed a massive effort for industrialization in a desperate attempt to catch up to the West. It became necessary to recruit many young people into the labor force, thus, they had postponed their educations. Nevena and Petar had married precipitously before he went off to the work camps.

But Petar had been outspoken about workers' rights and had led failed attempts to organize strikes. So, even though Bulgaria was slated to be more lenient than most communist countries, he had challenged the limits of their tolerance, and one day had simply disappeared. Nevena had not seen or heard from him in two years and could only assume he had died.

"It wouldn't be like him to make no attempt to communicate with me," she said. "Even prisoners are allowed to write home," she added, with a hint of resentment.

That explained how this beautiful person would be alone, trapped in this gray city, a victim of a gray world, an unfair world. I realized that for some, freedom comes easily, sometimes so easily that they abuse it or, incredibly, reject it. While for others, it comes at great cost and sacrifice.

The conversation fell momentarily into a reflective silence, so I asked her about the meaning of her name.

"Nevena," she explained, "is a flower; I think you would call it marigold."

How wonderful. I instantly recalled how my grandmother would set up altars on the day of the dead, a pre-hispanic celebration in honor of departed loved ones. These altars are traditionally adorned with the lively, orange cempazuchitl flowers; the marigolds that are native to Mexico.

Now feeling quite comfortable with each other, we were led with ease by the wondrous moment in which the burdens of living temporarily disappeared, and began talking more about ourselves; our origins, our beliefs, our aspirations, our sensitivities. We talked about music. We talked about friendship. We talked about love. We laughed.

Before we realized it, the café was closing, so she led me out of the restaurant, hooking her arm in mine, and we walked on happily, feeling the glorious effects of the wine, not caring about the icy, wintry night. Our friend in the trench coat was no longer there, and I figured that even communists knew how to create a space for lovers.

Nevena's apartment building was only a few blocks away. The whole time we walked, we were accompanied by a full moon, large and magnificent, knowingly watching us to light our way home.

6

The building was in dire need of reparations; it was a fading gray with patches of peeled paint. The hall was dimly lit, a floorboard was missing halfway up the stairs. When we reached the second floor, she stopped, and fumbling slightly with her keys, opened the door. Upon entering, she turned on the light and beckoned for me to follow.

It was surprisingly pretty inside, though cold. But once the space heater had kicked in, it began to feel cozy. The single light bulb blared brightly, but she turned it off once she had turned on the table lamp next to a cushioned chair – her reading chair, I surmised. The soft light, and the faint smell of lilacs, made the room quite relaxing. The walls were covered with beautiful paintings by some unknown artist (or were they hers?). There was a small dining table with four chairs next to the window, and against the opposite wall, a bed, neatly made with a bright blue and green quilt and two fat pillows. At the far end, there was a kitchenette. Above the stove were pale yellow cabinets. There was also a small bathroom with a curtain instead of a door.

Her nightstand was piled with books. In fact, books were everywhere; in orderly stacks on the floor or neatly placed in the single bookcase.

Nevena prepared some tea, and we sat at the table for a while without talking much, almost as if the moon had asked for our silence, imploring our admiration as she vainly showed off all her splendor through the windowpane. So, we turned off the lamp to fully draw in the moonlight.

I turned my eyes to look at Nevena, now enveloped in that magical light; precious in all her humanity. She looked at me in that captivating way once more, and a primal, yet tender urge flourished strong within my being. So, I took her in my arms and kissed her; lightly at first, then firmly, then passionately. We made our way to the bed, almost as if pushed by the moon herself, and slowly undressed.

We sought refuge, and warmth, under the covers, and we made love to the light of the moon that shone so intensely through the window; it was white and pure, and washed everything of its corrupt, gray dullness. The brightly lit objects on the table, casting playful shadows, almost came to life in an ethereal, magic moment of utter tranquility. We were lost in that light. Indeed, we were lost in time and space as we rose and fell in each other's arms in cadence to the rhythm of love.

Then…I slept. Oh, how I slept, now at home, in a universe of possibilities, of longings fulfilled, with the weight of her body pressing my side. I was no longer in the east or the west, but rather in a forbidden parallel reality, where all other persons, all things material, ceased to exist.

7

Morning had broken, and when I awoke she was looking down at me, already dressed for work. Her look was one of joy, and yet, there was a damp sadness in her eyes.

"Alberto, take me with you," she said. The softness in her voice made her request sound more like an idea than a plea. "We'll meet at the office, and I'll say I need to take care of something, and I'll get into the van and we'll go, yes? There are many obstacles, but I am willing."

I couldn't believe what I was hearing. Would she give up her small, meaningful possessions for me? True, she seemed awfully lonely, but was there something else driving her desire to flee? And I had completely forgotten about my companions back at the hotel. I knew they would guess what had happened, that I – true to the nature of a man – had succumbed to the enchantments of a beautiful woman. But what would they think about taking her along, at great risk of defying the local authorities? They surely did not have a need, an interest in doing so. They had not really known me for long, and yet, I felt our friendship had been sealed in the weeks we had traveled together, through thick and thin, in the adventure of our lives.

So, I said, as I stared into the ocean of her eyes, “Yes, Nevena, of course. We’ll meet and go, no matter what the cost.”

She kneeled next to the bed and kissed me. Then she did something no other woman had ever done or has done since; she touched my face, gently, lovingly, and I felt the vibrations, a soft oozing of love pass from the palm of her hand to my cheek.

Octavio Paz says ‘love is vertigo.’ Suddenly, I understood what he meant. At that precise moment, I felt a sweeping, spiraling force drawing me helplessly, yet sweetly, into a tumultuous vortex of emotions from which I knew, in that instant, I would never escape.

As she opened the door, a travel bag in her hand, she glanced back at me, smiling, and left. I didn’t know then that I would never see her again.

8

We parked in front of her office, everything on board the van, new tire mounted, and we waited…and waited.

Though reluctantly at first, my friends had accepted to bring her along, perhaps enticed by the promise of the added adventure it implied. For whatever reason, they were there, waiting with me. An hour passed, then ninety minutes. Another girl at the office had said she hadn't come to work. Where was she? I asked myself, beginning to feel desperation creep up inside me.

Then I saw him; our friend. His trench coat looked dirty in daylight, and he wore the same stupid sunglasses, a wire attached to an earpiece was now visible through his shirt collar.

"That guy looks suspicious," Manjeet said. "I'm afraid, my friend, she won't be coming."

What had he done to her? Where had they taken her? Was he stalking her because of Petar, or was she involved in something questionable on her own? I ran out of the van and crossed the street, yelling at him, demanding he tell me where she was. He raised a hand in a well-known gesture for me to halt, giving me a chance to back off. But I continued, rushing towards him, menacingly, blinded by so much uncertainty. He stood his ground and when I was sufficiently close, he smashed me squarely in the face with a fist that seemed to be made of stone. I was propelled backwards, feeling as if I were falling into a dark pit, hitting the bottom hard. I lay there dazed, looking up at a pale sky with swirling clouds. Was the sun really pink?

I staggered to my feet, like a fool, like a pugilist after a knockout punch. I faced him, and with an almost demented look on his face, he drew his gun and pointed…but did not fire. One last chance to let me go, I later figured.

Manjeet and Balbir took a huge risk and ran to me. Grabbing me by the arms and forcefully pulling me back.

“We have to go. Now!” Manjeet commanded.

I went limp in their grasp and fell into the van like a ragdoll.

9

All the way to the Turkish border, I thought of her and tried to muffle the sounds of my pain. Why had she not shown up? Had she changed her mind and didn't have the heart to tell me? Had she, perhaps, gone to say goodbye to her parents? Her friends? Had the police actually arrested her?

Or had her husband, by some enormous, unbelievable coincidence, appeared at the precise moment she was leaving for work? Incredibly, this crazy thought gave me solace, because I knew that at least, she would no longer be alone.

Yes, I imagined, even hoped, that Petar had inexplicably, miraculously survived after his disappearance, captive in some God-forsaken place, and upon hearing, through the endless thread of clandestine information known to occur amongst prisoners, that she was in danger, and thinking of her being subjected to torture or rape, and knowing now the ropes on how to obtain documents, and knowing also what guards were amenable to bribery, he had made a colossal, gargantuan effort to escape, fueled by an undying love, one that could break chains, move mountains, and with much more valor than I have, had gone to her rescue. He would at last lead her to safety, to France, or to England, or even to America.

Without knowing the man, in this wild, delirious scheme of mine, fed by bewilderment and a fecund imagination, we had become brothers, and had I met him then, I would have gone unto him with the words of E.E. Cummings as he spoke resignedly to his rival: "…accept all happiness from me. Then shall I turn my face and hear one bird sing terribly afar in the lost lands."

***

Now, I sit in the café where we dined that night, talking, laughing, peering into each other's eyes, and into each other's souls. I am sipping the same wine and pretending to eat the same soup, all the time thinking that, although I learned so much about her that night, things that were pressing, immediate, and even intimate, but I did not know enough of the things that could help me trace her; no family ties, no friends' names, no details of her birth. Indeed, I knew none of the things one knows about someone they love. So, I shall give up my search.

But the story has not ended. No love story ever ends; it simply remains forever adrift in a memory. It is a bittersweet memory of the woman that forever shall inhabit the sinews of my heart. And the image of Nevena in the moonlight will forever resurface whenever the cold wind blows, when the full moon shines, or when I hear cars honking as they make their way down a busy city street.

Spider's Web

For Mashi,
"For dreams too are a long road
whose end I will never reach."
– Yehuda Amichai

What an odd-looking place this is, thought Maiya as she sat there in the doctor's examination room. Dr. Joachim, an old-school psychoanalyst, had adorned his work place to purposely have an antiquated look; a glass cabinet with rocks and fossils, copies of Renaissance-era artwork on the walls, a bookcase with dusty, old volumes. But the highlight, Maiya mused – not without admiration – was a medieval tapestry on the wall opposite to where she was sitting, it prominently featured a unicorn poised on its hind legs, its mane fluttering in the wind, a crown of flowers on its head. And she understood why Dr. Joachim had placed it on his wall; this beautiful thing, Maiya sensed, provided tranquility to the already cluttered minds of his patients.

"What is it you most fear, Maiya?" asked Dr. Joachim, rather stiffly. His face revealed no emotion and he had asked this question with little commitment or true interest, or so Maiya believed – he was good at maintaining professional detachment.

Maiya pondered the question momentarily. "Spiders," she replied. "That is what I most fear."

Except for a barely perceptible wrinkling of his forehead and a slight rising of his right eyebrow, it seemed Dr. Joachim had not even heard her reply. But Maiya had picked up on the subtle signals and knew that he had.

"No, Maiya, what I mean is, what are the things in life that you fear? You know, such as loss of a loved one, lack of accomplishment, to fail in relationships, never finding love etc."

"Spiders," Maiya insisted. "You see, doctor, at everything that you have mentioned," she said, feeling her voice break and a sudden dampness in her eyes, "I have already failed. So, there is nothing else to fear at this point in my life, except spiders."

It was true. She had always been afraid of spiders. This fear began when she was very young, maybe eight or nine years old. It started while watching the movie, 'The Incredible Shrinking Man,' with her father, an enthusiast of vintage science fiction movies. The scene that most impressed her, and the ultimate cause of her arachnophobia, was when the shrinking man, now the size of a spool of thread, had to fight off a spider by wielding a sewing needle that, with great effort (it looked tremendously heavy for him, given his diminutive size), he eventually plunged into the spider's chest, killing it.

That night Maiya had a dream in which it was now she who had to fend off a giant spider after becoming ensnared in its web. She remembered, long after, the desperation at feeling the sticky threads of the web; they released a repulsive odor and the more she struggled to break free, the more entwined she became. It was all the more frightening because the whole time, the giant spider loomed close by, watching patiently with its multiple eyes that reflected the tenuous light in a sickly iridescence, waiting for her to become immobile. Indeed, it was silently waiting to impale her with its fangs and suck out the vital juices until there was no more essence of life left, leaving her a shriveled up, raisin-like carcass. The hideous aroma once again wafted down to her nostrils and she let out terrified screams for help, again and again! But no one came to her rescue. Luckily, she had woken up just in time, just when she could no longer take another breath; such was the grip the web had had on her chest, and yes, her very soul.

When Maiya opened her eyes, she saw her father leaning over her, his hand gently stroking her sweaty face and hair, whispering, soothing her with his gentle voice and crooked, loving smile. He had heard her screams and had come to her side to hold her as she sobbed into his T-shirt until the front of it was soaking wet.

It is fitting to say that this dream was symbolic of what life would be like for the girl; to feel small and meaningless, and endlessly falling into a spider's web – the snare of life, oppressive and unkind.

Or maybe it was more like wandering aimlessly through a labyrinth, each turn around each corner identical to the last, allowing her only fleeting moments of hope when she would glimpse the long-sought exit; a glimmer of light through the mist of emotions, a chance to finally end the suffering, end the struggle to remain afloat in the arduous task of self. But then it would close in its walls, bring down a black curtain, a lidless darkness, just as she had maneuvered its final turn. Once again, Maiya would feel lost and frightened because she could hear the scratchy footsteps of the spider advancing towards her through the darkened maze. And it would always be her father, even after she was already an adult, who would come to her rescue, time and time again. Quite simply, he believed in her.

It may seem odd to say that, despite everything, despite the bad dreams, Maiya had been a happy child. She was quick to smile, quick to relish in the humor of life, enjoying every minute, as she pondered on its meaning, even at that early age. There was a certain indefinable something about her – perhaps someone might call it charisma – that created a glow in everyone's heart.

She was also always playing pranks on her little brother in half-hearted attempts to gain attention. Basically, she was jealous of him for having removed her from her pedestal at the center the universe. But she did love him with an intensity that matched the intensity of life itself, and sometimes she would cry as her heart filled with a bittersweet feeling that became almost unbearable. That, too, can define what her life would be: fluctuations between happiness – almost euphoria – and a sadness very in tune with her boundless sensitivity. Everything in Maiya's life was, at once, a motive of both great joy and immense sorrow.

Maiya was growing up and was soon an adolescent who craved true friendship and becoming aware, little by little, of her own sexuality. There was a string of boyfriends, each one more complicated than the one before. In her deep feelings of low self-esteem, she always sought boys who didn't understand or deserve her. Not that they were bad people, they simply lacked the sensitivity, or better said, the fortitude to withstand the onslaught of Maiya's undulations in temperament – she was kind, yet demanding, and often unreasonable. So, they would leave her, often without a word, often in desperation.

We humans have our peculiarities, and one of them is that we reject what is obtained too easily. Thus, Maiya would reject the boys – and later the men – who would demonstrate true affection, always opting for the ones that were unobtainable or would mistreat her emotionally.

When Maiya was twenty-three, she was contacted by two childhood friends who were sisters and living in New Orleans, and with little coaxing, convinced Maiya to move there. They would be together, they said, and watch out for each other. After all, they were alone too – and struggling.

Maiya got a job as a receptionist at a hotel where in no time at all (she had no problem attracting men given her innate beauty and undeniable charm), she met a man. It was trouble from the start; a deception where he professed noble intentions – and love. But he was a user that drained her emotionally and led her fragile spirit to the edge of oblivion. Through all the failed attempts at love she had had, and all the partners that misunderstood her, no one had ever physically harmed her. This new 'love of her life,' troglodyte that he was, not only tired of the conflict, but revealing a true psychopathic penchant for cruelty, struck her with savage intensity, not once but several times, in the face, in the abdomen, leaving her bleeding from the nose, doubled over in pain, and feeling once again alone and intensely afraid.

Maiya remained in the hospital for a week, and as before, when she opened her eyes, she saw her father's face. He smiled at her, stroked her head, comforted her, spoke gently. Is there a greater, more unconditional love than what a father has for his daughter?

He took her home where she languished for a while, almost immobile, barely speaking, taking in the scenery of her childhood home; the majestic trees of the forest beyond the limits of the backyard, the garden with brightly colored perennial flowers, the smell of delicious meals cooking in the kitchen, the sound of rain pounding the tin roof in endless cacophony. Everything about the place brought back bittersweet memories of the past.

One night, Maiya, once again, had a dream about the spider. She found herself furiously and futilely fighting to unwind the hideous threads from her body. The putrid aroma once more stung her nostrils. She struggled to not look at the horrid arachnid poised overhead, breathing loudly, almost perversely, and laughing, it seemed. She felt weak and insignificant. But this time, she did not scream, did not cry out for help. She simply gave up the struggle, her mind giving way to a timeless resignation of body and soul. Strangely, in her surrender, now that she had lost all hope, she felt better.

And it was then that Maiya first tried to kill herself.

Maiya's thoughts had become unsound, giving way to the miasmic terror, but she didn't realize that the pills of the mild sedative she had taken in abundance would not have been enough to cause her death. And when she woke from her somnolence, she felt nauseous to realize that she had failed even in that.

Her sessions with Dr. Joachim began the following week, and Maiya, through a good measure of emotional catharsis – and effective medication – momentarily made progress and she went back to school and triumphed almost with no effort.

Once on her own, she floated from job to job. She felt most comfortable when working as a teacher; it was an opportunity to perform, act out (she loved acting), create a fantasy where she could expose to the world her happy nature, her love for life. But the unstable feelings began once more and the worm in her soul began to twist, gnawing a sinuous path through the deep tissues of her being.

The confusion began in earnest.

In her wanderings, in her attempts to find again the exit to the labyrinth, she came upon a man who, being as tortured as she was, took her on a journey through a downward spiral into a world of insanity and drugs. She tried, in brief moments of lucidity, to swim back to the surface, but the ocean of despair had a firm grasp – she was in too deep. She was untouchable and immune now; she was beyond access to acts of kindness. Love was a remote and faint memory, an absurd idea because, she thought, who could love her now?

She was more efficient in her next attempt to kill herself. She drew blood from her wrists with deep cuts. By the time her drugged up boyfriend had come to his senses sufficiently to know she was dying and had called for help, her organs were failing from the loss of blood that supplied vital oxygen; she was hanging on to life by a tenuous thread – one as thin and fragile as spider's silk.

Maiya had a lucid moment while in her hospital bed and she opened her eyes to realize that love wasn't dead. She, again, saw her father sitting there. He was weary, but nevertheless smiled.

"Don't you know, Maiya, that people that try to commit suicide are selfish?" he said, looking at her with tears in his eyes. "Your problems would be over but not those of the persons who love you and are left to live with pain and guilt."

Feeling ashamed, Maiya closed her eyes; she was overcome by exhaustion. When she woke, he was gone. On the nightstand next to her bed was a paper. She found the strength to pick it up, and through teary eyes, read what he had written.

Be wise, my little one,
With courage bear your ills,
For if you leave, there is no sun,
No smoky mist on snowy hills,
No baby smiling at those she trusts,
No ocean breeze or evening rain,
No glorious Earth or cosmic dust,
Just my soul left to wither in pain.

Asleep now, it was the spider again. It was peering down as before from the top of its web. But somehow, the look on its face was different; its mouth, surrounded by its multiple, glittering eyes, had the hint of a smile. It scrambled down suddenly towards Maiya and she felt afraid but unexpectedly courageous. Just as the spider was upon her, it stopped. After a brief pause, which filled Maiya with uncertainty, it lifted one of its front legs and gently stroked the cords of the web as if plucking the strings of a cello. And a beautiful, melodious sound emerged. With it, the cords of the web began to vanish, melting away into thin air.

Suddenly released, Maiya began falling, plummeting into oblivion, or so she thought. The initial terror gave way to tranquility, and once more to resignation – she knew she was going to die.

Maiya shut her eyes in anticipation of the fatal landing, but when she hit it was surprisingly soft. Thick vegetation seemed to cushion her fall and when Maiya touched the ground, she found she was able to stand up and bring her head and chest above the tall, tall grass; beautiful wild flowers of all colors imaginable were growing everywhere. She looked up at the sky and straight ahead, it was gray; maybe there was rain in the distance. But she felt warmth on her back so she turned around and squinted because the sun was shining and ablaze, wonderfully illuminating a baby blue sky, from somewhere a breeze with a hint of the ocean was blowing.

Maiya felt emboldened, and happily, with an unsuspected feeling of tranquility and relief, began to walk towards the glowing light.

Goethals Bridge

To Rilla – for what might have been.

"Say goodbye and say hello,
Sure enough, good to see you,
But it's time to go."
– James Taylor

Early spring evenings are made for riding country roads. So, that's what Mike and I did in the afternoons during those remaining months before graduation. His mother had a classy Chevy Super Sport that made you feel as if you were riding in the clouds. The windows would be rolled down and the warm breeze would soothe my face, mess up my hair – it created a sense of freedom and I felt alive and invincible, if only for the hour or two that we cruised.

Sometimes, when we didn't really want to go home, we would drive out to Surprise Lake. It was surrounded by a thick forest of maple and oak trees, the new spring leaves would shine in all the different tones of green imaginable. The water would be still but glittery as it reflected the waning sunlight. Small waves lapped the sand at the edge of the water where we would sit with shoes and socks off, smoking Tiparillo cigars while fantasizing about the girls we liked.

I had heard the term class struggle when Mr. Wheeler would lecture about economic theory and geopolitical crises, employing funny-sounding terms like: Malthusian, Marxism, dialectic materialism. But the only 'class struggle' I could understand was that of a working-class boy like me, Josh Rodriguez, struggling to be noticed by a high-class girl named Priscilla Klassen.

Oh, Priscilla smiled prettily and was polite and even laughed at my jokes. But, ultimately, she kept her distance.

So, she was what I would talk about as we smoked our cigars at the water's edge, our bittersweet conversation always accompanied by myriad chirping crickets heralding the night. A squadron of fireflies would magically appear and begin swirling about, blinking asynchronously, becoming palpable stars as they danced. It was as if the universe had suddenly contracted into a singularity, our personal space and time, a minuscule universe that was in proportion to our own small and meaningless selves. It was an immersion into a fantastical, dreamlike world that made me feel calm, large, and unafraid.

I am writing this from memory because I lost the journal I had kept for two years at the insistence of Miss Piroth, my English teacher, who said I had a knack for writing. She had suggested it only because she wanted me to organize my thoughts – a jumble of ideas as confusing as the times we lived in.

It was 1966 and there was much bewilderment. As we rode around, Bob Dylan would come on the radio and tell us, through his sentimental incantations, that the times they were a'changin'. We believed in our hearts that it was so. But we didn't really know how or in what way, only that it didn't seem to be for the better. We could see it all around us: youthful revolution, free love, drugs, and the cold war. People were living as if there would be no tomorrow. After all, Nikita Kruschev had stood before the whole world to say he would bury us – we didn't know exactly why. We Americans were oblivious to what was going on in the rest of the world – we had no need to know, so we were victims of our own success.

But in the midst of things – and center stage – was a real war raging in Vietnam. We were all fearful of being drafted and sent to fight a war we couldn't understand. We didn't even know where Vietnam was, much less what all the fighting was about. Our politicians told us, gravely, that the advance of communism had to be stopped in the name of freedom – it was our civic duty. Mr. Wheeler explained it more clearly, but in equally absurd terms. Communism was opposite to our system of government. Ours, known as capitalism, was based on democracy and free enterprise. In other words, based on the will of the people and their right to exploit other people in order to – at all cost – make money. Whereas, communism was totalitarian (another one of those funny-sounding words he used), a system in which the government had total control and told everyone what to do, and all citizens were neither rich nor poor. Truthfully, I didn't think it was such a bad idea. So, when he talked about this back then, my 17-year-old mind would wonder why on Earth it was so important for us to prevent communism from happening in that small Asian country. It seemed a simplistic and totally American idea. And American boys were returning severely injured, or worse, in body bags.

It was because of this that we decided to enjoy ourselves for as long as we could, or would be allowed. We were scared mainly of the uncertainty of what the future might bring, now that the war effort was in full swing.

So, Mike and I started venturing further out on our weekend excursions and would sometimes, with the intention of buying beer, drive to New York where the legal drinking age back then was still 18. To get from Summit, where we lived, to Elizabeth, the last city in New Jersey before entering New York, we would follow Morris Avenue almost to the end, then on to a knot of overpasses and eventually cross over the Goethals Bridge into Staten Island.

It only took about forty minutes to get there and with the requisite fake ID (we were both still underage, even in New York!), we could sit for a while in a bar, eat a burger, drink a beer. It was exhilarating to experience our first small steps at being independent.

One balmy spring evening, just two weeks before graduation, we were joined by our group of friends. So, there were six of us piled into Steve's station wagon that day. It was a neat vehicle that had plenty of cubbyholes to stash bottles. We were talking and laughing as we made our way across the Goethals Bridge.

I loved that bridge. My friends said it was an eyesore, but I could see beneath the rusty, sooty metal – blackened by decades of an endless stream of cars and trucks – a beautiful symbol of progress. Up close, it was nearly impossible to imagine how anyone could put together those huge steel girders in a tangible design, held together by jumbo rivets, almost as if a giant child had put it together with an Erector-set. It was exciting to hear the buzz of the tires on the metal road surface, its crescendo in proportion to our speed.

When we reached the land across the Arthur Kill, we veered left to Rocco's Tavern, about two more miles down the road. The evening was special; it was, perhaps, the last time we would all be together. Soon, after graduation and after summer was over, we would all go our separate ways, maybe never even see each other again.

All my friends were going to college. But not me. I had no idea when I would be able to continue my education. So, I decided I would get a job and maybe, over time, I would be able to enroll in the community college. My ascent into the ranks of the educated – having come from a line uneducated, yet hardworking people – would be a slow one. But I was determined that it would eventually be so.

But for now, I was thoroughly enjoying this outing with my friends, for whom I felt great affection.

We were at Rocco's for about two hours and stretching our limits, because after dark, the police would be suspicious of a group of boys out for no good reason other than to seriously defy the system in one last burst of fun before we had to face the reality of life after high school.

We left the bar almost tumbling over each other, but laughing nonetheless. As we crossed back over the bridge in the darkness, where the roadway became wide, there was a patrol car, its presence presaging an unwanted encounter with the law. As we passed, the dreaded flashing lights came on. So, Steve stopped and we waited while the sole policeman wrote down the license plate number then walked with exaggerated caution towards the car. He was straining to look inside as if searching for clues (of what, we didn't know).

His face was that of a kid not much older than us. It was a handsome face with youthful skin that still showed a few rebellious blemishes – you could tell he had had acne in his teenage years. The nametag on his left shirt pocket revealed his name: Joseph Pirelli.

He checked Steve's license and registration then looked inside at us, one by one, shining his flashlight in our faces. I was sitting in the back and was unable to suppress a giggle that emanated from somewhere in my nose with a snort.

"You've all been drinking, haven't you?"

How do you answer such an absurd, yet ironically accurate question? The major buzzing in my head brought on by the beer made me brave yet foolish.

"Wouldn't you if you were in our situation?"

"What do you mean?" he asked with an angry, yet perplexed frown.

"Well…we're worried about where we'll be in a few months' time when we're out of high school, with the war going on and everything," I added, now raising my voice in what I thought was a valiant way, "you should be ashamed of yourself."

The look on his face was that of a deer stunned by the bright light of a hunter. So I persevered.

"Have you stopped to think," I asked, "how unfair it is that we are not old enough to drink or vote and yet we are old enough to become soldiers and go fight some stupid war?" I was on a roll and laid it on thick. "By arresting us, or even scolding us, you become a participant of the enormous mockery of the politicians." I went on, now emboldened. “As an American who has sworn to defend justice, how do you feel about that?”

The question, surprisingly, laid heavily on his countenance in which I could detect a certain sadness. He turned and took a step towards his patrol car, paused, then turned to face me.

“Get out of the car,” he said, pointing at me.

“Why should I?”

I was appalled at how quiet all my friends were. Were they just afraid to speak up because it would get us into even more trouble, something that would certainly jeopardize their future plans? Or were they hating me for being foolish enough to defy an authority figure? Wasn’t precisely defiance what defined these crazy times of impetuous youthful revolution? So, why were they so quiet? Suddenly, I felt alone.

Officer Pirelli changed his tone. I could see his face now transformed almost into that of an understanding older brother.

So, I got out and walked with him to his car. He was taller than me, and muscular. And I realized that if there were to be a physical confrontation, I would be dead. Maybe I was too trusting, but the awkwardness of the situation had come to a head and it was do or die.

After an uncomfortable silence, with him looking down, at his shoes I guessed, he said, “You’re right, kid.”

Then, incredibly, his eyes became watery and he put his hand up to his face to stop the tears from trickling down his cheek, all the time turning away so my friends wouldn’t see he was crying.

"My kid brother, Bobby, the youngest in our family," he said, almost in a whisper, "was drafted eight months ago." He had no good reason to be telling me this, and it was obviously painful for him to go on, but he did.

"He was sent to that God-forsaken hellhole to fight and went missing two months ago." He was suppressing the trembling that accompanied this heart-felt speech. "Last week, we were notified that they had found his body. It could only be identified by his dog tags because…" he was really straining now to preserve a semblance of dignity, "his body was riddled with bullets and half burned."

He turned to me, his eyes swollen, embarrassed to have exhibited such a loss of composure, and barked, "Get out of here. Go straight home, I don't want to see you here again…you hear?"

I got back in Steve's car and we started back home.

"What was that about?" Steve asked. "It looked like that guy was having a breakdown."

"Nothing," I said. "He just decided to let us go, that's all."

"I'm glad, but why?"

I never answered him. In fact, I didn't speak again until I had gotten out of the car at my house and had said goodbye.

For the almost three months following graduation, I had been working at the Dairy Queen on Morris Avenue. It was an easy job but tiring, especially since I had offered to do extra shifts – they were understaffed and the manager liked me for it. But what the hell? I had nothing better to do for the moment. So, I became thoroughly immersed in this new task of making it in the working world.

On one particularly beautiful, late summer evening – the sky ablaze in pinkish-blue, as silhouettes stretched lazily along the pavement – near closing time, I heard a voice and knew instantly who it was, not only because it had that particular tone with which an individual can be identified, much as with a fingerprint, but also because it was the only voice that could create in me an ancestral calling, a primal reaction leading to the promise of love, manifested by an acceleration of my heart rate, and the total annihilation of reason.

"Hi, Priscilla," I said, hating that I could feel myself blushing. "What can I get for you?"

"Hmm, let's see. A small chocolate-dipped cone would be nice."

"Coming right up," I said, pretending to be calm, hiding the fact that I was struggling to avoid falling into the depths of her galactic blue-gray eyes. As I turned to the ice cream machine, I took a deep breath.

When I returned with her cone, she began rummaging through her purse, looking for her wallet. But I stopped her with a motion of my hand.

"It's on the house."

"Are you sure, Josh?" she asked. "You won't get into any kind of trouble, will you?"

"Nah, don't worry about that," I replied. "Besides, I won't be working here for much longer anyway."

"Why?" she asked with a genuine interest that surprised me. "Are you getting a new job?"

I hesitated before answering because of the knot in my throat. I gazed beyond her towards the street, barely noticing the passing cars.

"I've been drafted," I finally said. "I have to report to Fort Dix in two weeks. After that…I don't know."

"Oh!" The expression on her face revealed she had been stunned. She turned with cone in hand, walked a few steps, then sat down at one of the picnic tables and began eating her ice cream in silence.

As I began closing up the store, I noticed that, even after she had finished, she remained seated there, staring at the street, now dark and lighted only by the ghostly glow of the street lamp. She seemed, perhaps like I had been, oblivious to the passing cars and deep in thought.

I finished locking up and went to sit next to her on the bench. We were sitting without speaking for a while, then she looked straight into my eyes.

"They say you're a poet, Josh," she said. "Write a poem for me. Right now – one that I'll always remember."

I don't know where the inspiration came from (my mind always went blank when pressured or when I spoke before a crowd), but I guess it was the fact that I was finally alone with her on this beautiful night, taking in with all my senses the presence of her, a whiff of sweet perfume, the sheen of her skin, the sparkling in her eyes. There was a hint that the things that once could never have been – and that I longed for – were now possible; that this angel turned girl, turned young woman, was – for just this once – my wife. Compounding the pressure was the enormous burden of soon becoming a soldier, not knowing where I would go, whether I would live or die in a war as absurd as all the other wars that have existed in the history of humankind. I closed my eyes, breathed in deeply and the words came to me. So, before they would be lost, I quickly went back into the office of the Dairy Queen, repeating them in my head, and fetched a paper and pen.

When I sat back down next to her, I imagined I was already dead and that my spirit would fly to her side, where it would reside forever. And I wrote:

I wish to describe somehow with words
My love for you, but cannot lie,
I cannot find them for my love defies,
Description by plain and simple words.

So, if for love's sake, I should seek to cry
I wish that God not grant me words,
But make my voice more like that of birds,
And sing of you before I die.

When she had read it several times, she turned away and held her hand up to her face to wipe away tears that she didn't really try to conceal. We held on to a long pause.

"Josh," she said finally, with much tenderness, "will you write to me while we're both away? I promise I'll write back," she paused, then added, without doubt in her voice, "then we can see each other when we're both back in town."

"Yes, of course," were the only words I could muster – the knot was back in my throat.

Then she hugged me. It was a tight hug, bodies pressing against each, our scents mixing strongly in this unexpected encounter of love. Then, remarkably, she kissed me, full on the lips!

I had kissed other girls before and it had always been more experimental than anything, awkward moments of saliva exchange, fueled not by more out of curiosity than by lust; it was kissing without conviction. But it had never been like this moment with Priscilla; a kiss that mimicked the swirling summer leaves stirred by a warm, whispering wind, or stars leaving a bright trail as they revolved around Polaris…there was light…fire…ecstasy in her kiss!

She got out a piece of paper from her purse and borrowed my pen.

"Here," she said. "This is my address. My parents are having a going-away party for me, since next week I'm leaving for school. Will you come, Josh?"

I said I would try to make it – the smile on my face felt electric, stiff. It depended on work, I told her.

"Thanks," I said. But I knew I wouldn't go. Saying goodbye would be too painful.

A week later, I went to Staten Island by myself. No one else was around.

I went to Rocco's, as usual, but I had no one to talk to except the bartender on shift; all trivial things, the kind of things someone talks about to strangers. I missed everyone so, but they had all gone on their way, traveling down their own chosen road in life. I felt oppression in my heart, and once again, I felt alone.

As I made my way back across the Goethals Bridge – my bridge – I noticed a patrol car parked at a gas station. I was convinced it was Officer Pirelli whom I had thought about so many times since that spring day when, on this very spot, he had confided in me his sorrows. I had been grateful for it and felt a weird kind of friendship towards him. So, the urge to talk to him overtook me. I pulled right up next to the police car and got out. But as I approached, instead of Joseph Pirelli behind the wheel, I noticed it was a strange, chubby officer drinking coffee.

"Where's Officer Pirelli?" I asked, without bothering to introduce myself.

"Oh, him?" he responded, seeming momentarily confused. "Let me tell you, kid. That idiot quit the force about two months ago and joined the Army. What a screwball, on account of his being exempt and all." He went on. "He kept saying it was his civic duty, and that. What a bunch of crap." He paused, making sure I was listening. "And now he went and got himself killed," he added in a brutally mocking tone.

"What?" I asked in total shock.

"That's right. The bastard didn't even last a week. The freakin' Viet Cong, or whatever you call them, took care of him mighty quick." And he laughed a painfully stupid laugh.

"Don't talk about him like that!" I yelled. I couldn't stand the sight of this brutish imp of a man.

"Hey, what's it to you anyway, kid?" he asked. "You a relative of his or somethin'?"

For a while, I stood there dumbfounded. Then the revolution in my gut stirred in me a helpless feeling. So, I walked back to my car and took out the bottle liquor I had purchased. And with tears in my eyes, walked to the curb and smashed it right in front of the patrol car.

"Hey!" blurted out the stupid policeman behind the wheel. "What'd you do that for?"

I turned to look at him, the fury building up inside. I wanted to curse at him for being so insensitive. I wanted to punch him in the face with all my might. I wanted to hurt him and make him feel everlasting pain. But there had already been enough hurting going on in the world, I figured.

I felt the weight of Joseph Pirelli's death squarely on my shoulders, and that of his kid brother, and that of all the American boys who had already died or would be dead in the near future. Indeed, on my shoulders lay the enormous burden of senseless death; death that so affected all of humankind during warfare, and I thought of how the existence of aggression and conflict that is so prevalent in the natural world affects all living things, even humans. We're all bound to it by a necessity to survive. Life is hard, and complicated, so I didn't – I reasoned in a matter of seconds – want to make it any more complicated than necessary by showing my own aggression towards the policeman; it would not be worth it. He had, after all, impressed me as brutal and non-thinking – alas, he was a survivor.

So, I counted to ten, let the fury quell, walked up to him and loudly answered his question, almost yelling in his face.

"Because...I'm too young to drink!"

Priscilla's Last Letter

I found, or thought I found, you did exceed
That barren tender of a poet's debt;
And therefore have I slept in your report.
– William Shakespeare

Dear Josh,

I read your letters again today. I remember hoping that you would come back some day and find me. I was always anxious for you to hold me in your arms and whisper your sweet words into my longing ears. But it was never to be.

In your last letter (oh, Josh, I know it by heart), you told me that you were in a tent in camp, writing hurriedly, shells striking at random, stupidly hoping to hit some unknown target, with gunfire ever present in the distance. Your feet were damp – the rain seemed endless in Vietnam, you wrote.

You said the last time your platoon went out on patrol, you were ambushed. Five of the men died. You held Eddy – the buff Texan boy who had become your best friend – as the warm blood from his body soaked your shirt and you felt his life wane, his being struggling to remain amongst the living, even when that would be impossible. He had sustained mortal wounds to his body, but hopefully, not to his soul, you thought with despair. The injuries had been made by that unseen enemy – it was like fighting ghosts, you said. You wrote a poem about it; you needed to express the horrific feelings churning inside your being. I remember it because I have read it many times:

I saw my friend die today, he drowned,
But it was not the sea that covered him,
The sea is far away.
He drowned, nonetheless,
Asphyxiated by the sea inside him,
It gushed up filling his lungs,
It took hold of his very soul,
Which hesitated, then left to who knows where?
The injuries and pain were far too strong.
I've seen other men die, as well,
Blown apart for no good reason,
Men on our side, men on the other side,
We'd look into each other's eyes,
Blow each other apart,
Destroy what the universe took so long to perfect,
Blew each other apart, but there was no hate,
There was only confusion,
Different only by geography,
But, ultimately, equal in death.

I wrote back to you, Josh, the very instant I read that letter, even though you probably didn't receive my reply until much later, if at all – the Army, it seemed, had trouble finding you in the front.

If you never got a chance to read it, here is what I wrote: "Come back to me that I might give you the kisses that I long to give you, that I owe you for all the years your love has been dedicated to me."

Even after all these years, after I found out you had been reported 'missing in action,' and after the dreadful confirmation that they had found your body in a ditch in some infernal place, yes, even long after I finished college and worked in an accounting firm, and finally married (at the age of 38), had children, and my children had children...I read your letters. Your letters, Josh, were the lifeline to all that in life is good, and beautiful and true.

I keep your letters, Josh, in a place that only I know of, away from prying, critical eyes.

But even if by some horrible calamity, they were all destroyed, it doesn't matter because they have, for years, and by shear memory, been locked away in that secret place only a woman can know of, because that is her prerogative...to have a secret of the heart.

Part of my secret, Josh, is that I hide a treasure, a cherished possession. It is the piece of paper on which you wrote one day, in a flash of inspiration, fueled by a love so great it could redefine the human species. We are beings evolved to such a degree that we acquired the capacity to feel a love that can defy explanation, a love as you always had for me...and I for you.

I have unfolded and folded back that piece of paper you gave me in 1966 so many times that it is torn at the edges and in the middle. But what can you expect from a paper that is fifty years old!

You wrote on it that miraculous poem of love, a poem for all the centuries, a poem for me. And in so doing, you made me the luckiest woman in the world. And when I read it, and I have done so countless times, it has the ability to make me soar over windy seas, traverse sandy deserts, scale the jagged, icy cliffs of terrifying, dark mountains; all in search of a tender rendezvous of love. In life, you see, Josh, there has always been just you and me.

Last month, I went to Staten Island over the Goethals Bridge to visit a relative of my husband's. I have gone over that bridge many times, and yes, I know it is *your* bridge.

Soon after you left for the war, I ran into your friend, Mike, and he told me the story about your fascination with that bridge, how you found beauty in it, imprinted for all the ages by the marvelous feat of building it, and how it bespeaks the triumph of the human spirit and humankind's will to transform the world in a positive manner. It is so at odds with the ugliness of waging war and creating death, you said. It was so like you, Josh, to find beauty in everything, even when there is ugliness as well.

When we got out of the car that day at Staten Island – at the relative's house – I was helped by my husband. He is a good man, Josh, and has treated me decently, although he is insensitive to my needs. He is a good provider, but not really loving in the true sense of the word. Perhaps I am being unfair, but he never really touched my heart as you have. But life has a way of dictating when it is time to realize that if you cannot have what you want, you must find what you need. And so, I have settled for a good man who has been able to give me a comfortable life and the children in which to invest the joy of loving for the rest of my life. Anyway, as I was saying, when we arrived at his cousin's house, he helped me get out of the car and into my wheelchair. Yes…I cannot walk.

I was diagnosed with breast cancer four years ago. My doctors kept it at bay for a while, but eventually, it came back and invaded my bones. The most severe consequence has been that it went to my spine and ever since, I have been paralyzed from the waist down. My oncologist has been honest with me – the situation does not look good.

My consolation, dear Josh, is that soon I will see you again. Where? As you say, one cannot know for sure; it will be where Eddy's soul went, I presume. Some people call it heaven, others the afterlife. Still others see it as an indefinable realm where substance and the insubstantial are one, a place where form doesn't matter, only spirit. Perhaps, it will be in some parallel universe where we have already been together all this time, whereas in this universe, we were not so lucky.

At any rate, I will soon find out. So, I am finalizing this, my last letter to you, by saying: "Soon, my love. It will be sooner rather than later."

With all my love,

Priscilla.

The Night of Panchito Che

"I'm tired of weeping and the dawn doesn't come."
From the song *Paloma Negra* by Tomás Méndez

As I drove along, the engine of my tiny Volkswagen began to churn happily. It was letting me know of its contentment that the going from that moment on would be downhill.

It deserved a break after struggling up the steep hills and navigating the twists and turns of the highway, traveling against the wind, as it made its way through the cordillera of Chiapas. I had left San Cristobal de la Casas sixty minutes earlier and what would have been of a journey of 80 kilometers – as the crow flies – became much longer because of the sinuous road. But the beauty of the land more than made up for the added travel time.

The mountains were covered by an alpine forest. In some places, the peaks were so high they perforated the clouds that lay lazily in the void as if refusing to go home. In some places at the edge of the road, next to the bus stops, there are indigenous people clad in colorful, home-woven garments selling their wares: an incongruous mixture of handicrafts, forest orchids, and bottles of Coca-Cola on ice.

A sharp curve at the edge of a perilous cliff let me see the city of Tuxtla Gutiérrez far below, sprawling ungamely through the valley, like a blemish. Everything was white;

the houses, the buildings, the treetops. This was the illusion created by the intense sunlight in this land where the sun reigns supreme.

It was still early in the afternoon, but when I finally arrived and had worked my way through the city traffic to my apartment, I closed the curtains, crawled into bed, shut my eyes and sank into a deep sleep, a peaceful oblivion.

When I awoke, the hot, hot day had finally given way to the refreshing breezes of the night. And, as happens almost daily in these southern reaches of Mexico, the night people of the city, allured by the pleasant temperature and the prospect of fun, began wandering towards Main Street where life began anew after sunset.

Following a renovating shower and a change of clothes, I went in search of my friends. That night promised to be special because José Luís and Mina were visiting from Mexico City and staying with their longtime friends, Iván and Hilda.

When I arrived at their house, Ivan's cousin, Checo, and his wife, Toyi, were also there, greeting me warmly – two handsome people with handsome smiles. They were happy to join us, they said.

As we were leaving, Paco arrived. He and I had moved simultaneously to Tuxtla Gutiérrez and worked together, similar situations in our lives had made us close friends. We were both trying to turn the page on our troubles.

So, there were eight of us that night, ready to explore, listen to music, happy to be together on that beautiful summer night.

Our wanderings led us to the newly opened El Nucú Bar in the María Eugenia Hotel, just off of Calle Central. As we walked in, the lights were dim and the air thick with smoke. There was a live band playing; a South American group stepping loudly and happily through a piece extracted from somewhere in the Andes Mountains.

We sat down in a corner, to one side of the platform stage – it was the only space big enough for a party of eight – squeezing in three little, round tables with the aid of a waiter who asked us to watch our step since the cables of the sound equipment were strewn on the floor and in our way. As I moved in last, I accidently nudged the bombo player with my elbow. But he turned to me with a smile and nodded without ever losing his timing.

Glasses, two bottles of brandy, a bucket of ice and six medium-sized coca-colas were promptly delivered to our tables. I was impressed that Iván had, quite ably, ordered these items as we were working our way into our seats.

And the party began.

By the time the first round of drinks and the appetizers were finished, the South Americans were in their finale, tenderly singing a bittersweet song that alluded to some unavoidable facts about Latinos: although we walk amongst the living, we talk to the dead – our dead ancestors who were misunderstood and mistreated. Their blood remains on our hands as a constant reminder of our martyrdom. And yet, there is hope, for we descend from ancient kings and we all sustain in our hearts the certainty that each and every one of us is of noble birth.

The last notes strummed dramatically on the charango, and as the hearty applause erupted there was a collective feeling that by some strange, undefined wisdom, we were all applauding ourselves.

The band left and the lights of the stage went out, leaving us suddenly in semidarkness. The sound of voices in a hurry to speak commenced in a crescendo and added to the noise of the clinking glasses. We had an animated conversation with José Luís and Mina, whom we had not seen in a long time. We gossiped about the political and social world of Mexico City – the great metropolis that defies definition but that we all loved – and we laughed with gusto upon hearing the recent political jokes circulating around the capital.

Suddenly, the lights on the stage came back on, momentarily blinding us. The MC stepped up and introduced the next act; more music and songs, but this time from a solo performer, Gerardo Arias, an accomplished artist that even had a successful recording contract and a fairly well-known song that was working its way up the charts.

The crowd received him warmly and he began his performance. But it soon became evident he would be having a bad night because his guitar playing was off key and his voice lacked the strength to hold the prolonged notes. I could detect a certain slurring of words, since the lyrics, even of his well-known songs, were incomprehensible. I suspected he had been drinking. We all looked at each other with more embarrassment than annoyance, and I hoped he would not have long repertoire planned for that evening – it was painful to watch.

Still, he sang for about forty-five minutes more; by then, the crowd had already lost interest. When he announced his last song, a few spectators almost cheered.

It was a well-known and beloved song in Mexican folklore entitled 'Sigo Siendo El Rey' (I Am Still the King). Once again, it seemed appropriate; although you have lost love, money, friendship, and your way in life, you can still feel regal in spirit. So, we applauded, once again, unwittingly to ourselves when his performance finally came to an end.

To our surprise, he did not step down and remained on the stage, looking around, trying to focus beyond the glare of the lights.

"Tonight," he said, "in the crowd, there is someone who has asked for an opportunity to sing. And even though I have heard him during the many times we have practiced together, he has not yet had the opportunity to perform in public." Gerardo stood up and waved at someone, beckoning him to step forward.

"So, may I introduce to you, ladies and gentlemen, the one and only Panchito Che!"

A curious stage name, I thought. And it fit the character perfectly. From his chair at a front row table across from us, we saw the improbable Panchito Che stand up. He was short, with a beer-belly and wore baggy pants. His Fu-Manchu mustache contrasted starkly with his pudgy, baby face. The way he wore the long collar of his white shirt, on top of the lapels of his navy-blue sports jacket, added to this boyish image and he had a serious – almost frightened – look on his face. All this made him seem not unlike a child stepping up to his first communion.

Panchito Che walked shyly forward without making eye contact with anyone and jumped onto the stage. As he sat down on the tall stool, he began adjusting the microphone in a manner that someone with stage fright does in order to buy some time and size up the crowd. Gerardo personally handed him his own guitar.

After a prolonged, awkward silence, during which he fiddled with the strings of the guitar, he began speaking. Panchito's voice was shaky as he spoke with lots of throat-clearing. It also revealed that he probably had also begun drinking since quite early that evening. Nevertheless, he was sober enough to be nervous about having finally been brought before a live audience.

When he began to play, the nervousness and the effects of the alcohol vanished as if by magic and an entirely different persona emerged; one of an accomplished artist whose demeanor hinted at a bohemian lifestyle. And out there in the spotlight, he seemed a million miles away.

He chose a tender love song to begin his act. And his voice became deep and voluminous – and spectacular! It was the kind of voice that, if discovered and nurtured, might well have led Panchito to a career in opera.

He delivered song after song in a style that was both captivating and unique. Upon completion of each song, Panchito's timid and gracious bows were met with raucous applause and the clapping became progressively louder and prolonged until it was accompanied by enthusiastic and repeated cries of 'BRAVO!' An hour went by and we were still captivated by his talent.

A stunned Gerardo watched uneasily from the chair that Panchito had vacated. He had not expected Panchito's performance to be so inspired when his own had been so dismal. He had been shown up and outdone and he resented it. The anger in his eyes began to rise and I thought how transparent one can become in situations of anger or envy or guilt.

Gerardo got up from his chair and stood in front of Panchito and began addressing the crowd with an abundance of hand gestures.

"Thank you very much, but Panchito has to leave now," he yelled. He then tried to take his guitar away from Panchito.

"NOOO!" was the unified reply, followed by, "ENCORE, ENCORE!" Panchito Che stood his ground, steadfast like a rock and gripped the neck of the guitar tightly. So, Gerardo momentarily backed off and Panchito sat back down on the stool.

He told us he would be pleased to sing us one more song and then call it a night.

From the moment he began to sing, nostalgia and longing flowed through me like a river, a torrent of emotions. He had chosen, as his encore, a sad song entitled 'Paloma Negra' (Black Dove), a heartbreaking narrative about lost love. It wasn't exactly because of the particularly intense manner in which he sang it, eyes closed, almost in a trance, as if savoring the words that – I wondered – he might be identifying with, it was more the particular moment in my own life, full of sadness and confusion, that brought the emotions hurtling back at me, making me feel an overwhelming fatigue.

What came instantly to mind was the last time I had heard that song. Paco and I were on one of our frequent nighttime rides in his yellow Volkswagen Rabbit around the Tuxtla Gutuiérrez bypass; we liked getting out for a while, feel the warm, summer air, quell the fire inside and listen to music as it blasted on the stereo. That night, Mari Toña was with us.

She and I were good friends and were in love, just not with each other. But there we were, both of us lonely, so we often sought each other's company.

It is said that there can never be close friendship between a man and a woman without it becoming intimate; ultimately, the tyranny of sex will break down your resolve and you can no longer remain just friends. And that someone falls in love seems inevitable. One of two outcomes can occur: either the friendship ends under the pressure of unrequited love, or it thrives with the other reciprocating that love.

But all Mari Toña and I knew was that, at that particular moment, on that particular sultry night, we were happy to be together and squeezed into the passenger seat of Paco's car listening to music.

Suddenly, 'Paloma Negra' played on the radio. I felt Mari Toña lean heavily into me and put her head on my shoulder as the three of us began to sing along. I could feel the softness of her body against me, could smell her perfume as it drifted upward in a gentle mist. I put my arm around her shoulders. She and I closed our eyes as we sang softly. Paco, on the other hand, was singing at the top of his lungs. His eyes seemed to be tearing up; he had recently lost his wife.

The laments of eternal love reverberated as the radio played and as we sang. But we were singing, not only to the loss of love between a man and a woman, but also to losing the love of beauty, love of oneself, and the love of living.

A week later, Mari Toña left town without saying a word. I thought I had come to know her, understand her moods and desires, her girlish longings, felt her pain as if it were my own. But she had plans that didn't include me. I only wish I had had the chance to tell her how much that night in Paco's car – and she – had meant to me.

Back at the Nucú Bar, while Panchito Che was in his sentimental rendition of the beautiful song, I glanced at Paco and saw that he, too, was smiling the happy yet sad smile of one who has been touched emotionally, the smile of one devastated by memories.

The applause was explosive; the vibrations within the enclosed quarters shook the glasses that trembled and rang faintly. The screams of 'BRAVO...BRAVO' became louder and more insistent than ever.

As Panchito stood up to bid farewell with a timid bow, the crowd began to roar and simultaneously, in unison, led on by some invisible instruction, started chanting, plainly and simply, but loudly, "PANCHITO ...PANCHITO ...PANCHITO..." all the time banging on the tables.

Panchito Che stood immobile, intrigued by his own success. Gerardo also stood up, sharply, with an angrier look than before and attempted to retrieve his guitar from Panchito, who seemed lost in wonder.

We booed Gerardo over and over again, then began to, once more, demand an encore. "ENCORE...ENCORE..." we cried, letting it all out, letting go, partly prompted by the drinks and partly by our natural emotions. A near riot ensued.

An especially rowdy group across from us stood up on the tables and began throwing napkins and peanuts at

Gerardo, who seemed defeated. The hotel manager appeared before us, working his way to the stage.

"Please calm down," he implored. "You are disturbing the hotel guests. We ask that you please proceed to the exits since we are now closing." He had already turned on the house lights.

"NO!" was the reply in a single angry voice.

Prompted again by some invisible power, some people rapidly approached Panchito and raising him on their shoulders began victoriously parading him around the room. The cries of 'PANCHITO...PANCHITO...' once again rang out.

The crowd did eventually simmer down. After about fifteen minutes of this outrageous spectacle, everyone seemed to be regaining their composure. One by one, as they were leaving – speaking excitedly, wide smiles on their faces – went over to congratulate Panchito on his incredible performance, with lots of backslapping and hugging.

Iván and Checo weren't ready to call it a night. Suddenly, they engaged Panchito in a lively conversation. They informed us that Panchito Che was coming home with us; they had offered to pay him one thousand pesos for a personal performance at Iván's house. Some people we didn't even know had overheard and asked Iván if they could tag along; they were willing to contribute another thousand pesos – such was their enthusiasm for Panchito's singing.

So, as we left the bar at one o'clock in the morning, the party of eight had swollen to nearly twenty persons.

Upon arrival, Iván opened the doors wide to let everyone in. We all volunteered to rearrange the furniture (under Hilda's direction) to create a makeshift stage. Iván also opened his personal bar to everyone. Ice cubes clanked, glasses tinkled, beer cans swished, laughter rang out. He then retrieved a guitar from a closet beneath the stairs (a cousin of his had left it behind one day) and handed it to Panchito along with a tall drink.

Panchito took his place on one of the tall barstools, sipping his drink, tuning the guitar, clearing his throat, sipping his drink again. With a flare of drama, he remained perfectly still – there he was, playing star again.

His singing was good once more, his voice was still strong, his guitar work technically impeccable. But something was different. It took me a while to figure it out – the spontaneity was gone!

Panchito Che was now trying too hard.

I began to feel weary. The day's events had started early in the morning – the stress of the business meeting, the lunch with difficult clients, the road trip home on a difficult highway, the late-night excitement at the bar – and they had taken a toll; I decided to close my eyes for just a moment.

When I opened them again, the guests had already left. Iván and Hilda were not around. The lights had been turned off except for a small lamp on an end table next to couch where I had fallen asleep. Someone had covered me with a quilted afghan. Only Panchito remained. He was curled up in an armchair, his clothes all wrinkled, hair disheveled, mouth wide open and snoring lightly. He seemed a small and sad figure, maybe even pathetic, I recall thinking.

In life, we all have our fifteen minutes of fame, they say; a moment when we are launched into sudden, unexpected glory, only to be brought back down cruelly, once that moment has passed, to our earthly condition. For most of us, that moment of joy shall never be repeated, no matter how hard we try.

I got up and walked to the door and as I opened it, I had an inclination to look back at Panchito Che, but decided not to. I didn't want to remember him in that state. I much preferred to recall forever how he had looked during his night of triumph; he had momentarily been the conqueror of our hearts and minds – he had dominated the world through his art and had bestowed a gift: that of having witnessed a rare and heroic moment of artistic excellence when we – and the artist himself – had least expected it.

These thoughts made the walk home a little lighter. The sun was busy in its task of bringing the dawn, its yellow-pink light far in the distance above the hills. A cool morning breeze was blowing and I felt invigorated at the thought of a new day.

Acknowledgments

I wish to thank the many friends that read one or more of the stories before their completion. They enlightened me with their wise suggestions and made, I believe, the stories better.

First and foremost is Pete Zupan, my longtime friend, who would return the printed copy of the stories, one by one, full of marginal notes and commentaries. Eduardo 'El Chori' López Corella, mentor, friend, and always an inspiration, also took time out of his busy day to give me his thoughts. The journalist and artist, Enrique Chao, also a longtime friend, and the writer and illustrator, Joan Hellquist, whom I have known since high school, both provided me with constant encouragement. Honorable mention goes to my dear friends, Raúl Garza and Tomás García. Thanks also to Javier García, Gabriel and Adriana Rosales, and Mike Pedicini (the Mike from Goethals Bridge).

Lastly, thanks to my family for loving the idea of writing my stories.

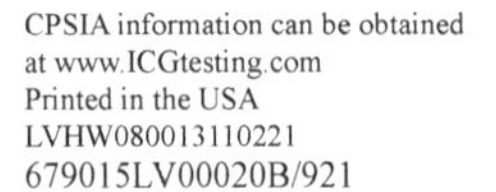

CPSIA information can be obtained
at www.ICGtesting.com
Printed in the USA
LVHW080013110221
679015LV00020B/921

9 781643 782157